Past
the
Dark Field

Sheila van den Heuvel-Collins

for the blue bird

Fifty percent of the author's proceeds from this book will be donated to MAP-supporting projects and research.

Table of Contents

Glossary

anti-contact (anti-c): a person who accepts that children cannot consent to sexual acts with an adult (see *non-offender* and *VirPed*)

AoA: Age of Attraction (age range to which the person is attracted)

BL = Boy Lover

child molester: a person who sexually abuses children

CL = Child Lover

CSA: Child Sexual Abuse; Child Sexual Abuser

CSEM = Child Sexual Exploitation Material

dox: to make personal information or private identity public

ephebophilia = attraction to ages 15-16 (or legal age of consent; frequently to age 19)

exclusive = only attracted to children

ex-offender: a person who has molested, fulfilled their judicial sentence and resolved to not offend again

GL = Girl Lover

hebephilia = attraction to ages 11-14

hentai = animated or illustrated pornography (film or book)

loli (short for **lolicon**) = animated or illustrated prepubescent girls in hentai

MAP: Minor-Attracted Person

nepiophilia (sometimes **infantophilia**) = attraction to ages 0-4

non-exclusive = attracted to adults as well as children

NOMAP = Non-Offending Minor Attracted Person (considered offensive by some, as they object to the need to state they've never committed a crime)

non-offender: a pedophile who has never molested a child (see *anti-contact* and *VirPed*) and has never used child sexual abuse images (CSEM)

pedophile: a person whose sexual attraction includes minors (Greek: pedo = child, phile = friendly lover)

pedophilia = attraction to ages 4-11

pro-contact (pro-c): a person who believes society is mistaken in assuming children cannot consent, and that children are able to consent if properly instructed in sexuality

shota (short for **shotacon**) = animated or illustrated prepubescent boys in hentai

teleiophilia = attraction to adults

VirPed: Virtuous Pedophile (see *non-offender* and *anti-contact*)

MAP Chat: Introduction

NotYourMother:

The rules:

1. You **must** be committed to **never engaging in sexual activity with a child.**
2. No admissions of unadjudicated illegal activities. This includes breaking your local child pornography laws. If you have participated in illegal activities, please turn yourself into the authorities.
3. No talk about lowering AoC (Age of Consent) no matter where you live.
4. No pro-contact talk. If you want to change society's attitudes towards child sexuality, this is not the place for you.
5. No images or videos of real children in any state of undress or sexually-suggestive poses. If a MAP might find it attractive, don't post it.
6. No sexually-explicit or arousing description of any kind is permitted.
7. Protect your identity. Don't use the same avatar or user-name on any other sites. Don't describe anything related to your real identity. Don't upload

images that might be geo-tagged or that might allow someone to identify you.

NotHumbert: Thats a lot of rules

NotYourMother: My way or the highway

NotHumbert: Didnt say they were bad rules

NotYourMother: If you dont like them find another MAP chat

PedoProud: I think they're quite good. They make me comfortable. Besides, most of the chats have similar rules.

NotYourMother: Feel free to introduce yourselves

PedoProud: I'm PedoProud. I'm a twenty-something woman. Non-exclusive hebephile GL. Out to one friend and my mother. Friend is helpful; mother is not.

NotHumbert: Late twenties trans f-m

Nonexclusive pedo hebe ephebo gl

Out to my therapist

GimmeLolita: Creepin' up on middle age mother of four nonexclusive nepio pedo hebe

Ephebo is too old for me

After 13 give me adults

Out to my husband and sister and best friend and a therapist.

NotYourMother: @GimmeLolita that user name breaks rule #1

Change it

GimmeLolita: She was a fictional character

NotYourMother: Dont care

DontGimmeLolita: Fine

Changed it

NotHumbert: Do you like the book?

DontGimmeLolita: Love it

u?

NotHumbert: Nah. unrealistic

PedoProud: @DontGimmeLolita Which gender?

DontGimmeLolita: cl they all look good to me

PedoProud: No one is exclusive.

Oskar: I am exclusive.

DontGimmeLolita: Who are you?

Is Oskar you're real name like the Grouch

Oskar: You are not the first person to ask me that question. No. I am not yet decomposing, and I am only a little grouchy.

I am a senior. I am an exclusive pedophile and hebephile boy lover.

DontGimmeLolita: Why are u a little grouchy

Oskar: That is the result when one goes one's whole life without any sexual relations.

bunnyboy: u gone ur whole life without sex

like 65 years

Oskar: My life has been much longer than that, young person.

bunnyboy: holy shit

NotYourMother: No profanity

bunnyboy: sorry i mean wow

Oskar: That is the opinion of youth: that it is impossible to avoid sexual activity. It is possible.

PedoProud: Was it a choice? Did you ever try adults?

7

Oskar: I am exclusive. The choice is between celibacy and child sexual abuse.

bunnyboy: i thought making it halfway through my teens was bad

DontGimmeLolita: Who are u @bunnyboy?

bunnyboy: midteens nonexclusive nepiopedo bl not out

    taking this shit to my grave

    sorry

    *stuff to my grave

NotHumbert: @bunnyboy you're young

bunnyboy: ur anticontact

    im safe

NotHumbert: Yes i know

    you're in no more danger than any other kid

Oskar: There are myriad anti-contact websites which forbid minors. If anyone is uncomfortable with the presence of minors, they may participate in a different chat. We will give you a list to choose from.

DontGimmeLolita: @bunnyboy how did u get here if ur not out?

bunnyboy: @NotYourMother headhunted me

   i made a comment on a youtube video that coulda got me in trouble

DontGimmeLolita: Good on ya @NotYourMother

bunnyboy: no one gonna ask what he was doing looking at that video

Oskar: He was recruiting young boys for a life of no crime.

bunnyboy: @Oskar how do you know

Oskar: I have been friends with Not Your Mother for some years now. We met on a different anti-contact website.

NotHumbert: Youre friends in person

Oskar: No, of course not. We have never met. We do not even know the other's real name or what he looks like. I do not think we are even in the same country. English is not my first language. He is fluent in English.

PedoProud: That's kind of sad—that you've never met. Not the English thing.

NotYourMother: Safety first

PedoProud: I understand that, @NotYourMother. It's just kind of sad that you can't even video chat.

Oskar: Loneliness is a thing I am now used to.

bunnyboy: shit

NotYourMother: No profanity in the group chat

bunnyboy: shoot

Karl

Monday

The neighbours to the left of Karl's house went away for the weekend. They pulled out of their driveway just after 9 a.m. Their house has been quiet since then.

Karl notes their return on Monday evening, just after dinner. Through the slats in his blinds, he watches the figures in the driveway.

Tuesday

It's an unextraordinary day of July heat and sun, the first official day of the summer vacation. As his mother scuttles around, getting ready for work, Karl is informed of his options: clean his room or paint the garage door.

He flings a bare leg over the arm of the easy chair and hits pause on the game controller. "What's with the medieval parenting approach?"

His mother digs in her briefcase. By the purse of her lips, he guesses she's counting to ten. "You're not spending the summer doing nothing. You'll get depressed and then anxious, and we'll be in the same boat as last year. I'm sorry you didn't get either of the camp jobs, but we could certainly use your help around here."

"That's why you had me, right? Slave labour?"

"Yes."

Her lips are starting to get thin; he raises an eyebrow at her.

"I've left a list of things to do, as well as the big chore of your choosing. Dad'll be home around 6:00, so it would be nice if you had dinner ready for 6:30. I've got a late client so I won't be home until 8:00. Save me some food."

"Yes, ma'am!"

"Karl..."

"Yes, Mother, I will do the required chores. You may go to work confident that I won't kill too many zombies or retire to my boudoir in a vale of tears."

"You might also make some social arrangements for yourself."

"Tea party on Thursday. Yep."

"Child...."

"Adult...."

She walks over to kiss his forehead and smooth his hair off his face. "Text me if you need anything—and put the groceries on the credit card. Love you."

"Love you, too."

He decided, a couple of weeks ago, to tread lightly this summer; he won't give his parents an excuse to ask too many questions, to pay close attention. When he hears the car pull away, he gets up to examine the list of tasks.

Immediately, he changes his gym shorts and Real Madrid jersey for American Eagle shorts and a short-sleeved button-down that he'd ironed while his parents slept in the day before. He combs his hair and checks to make sure he's applied deodorant.

Even with the wind cooling his face as he zips his bike along the suburban streets, his shirt sticks to his skin beneath the backpack. He pedals a little faster.

In the grocery store, the people smile at him as they walk by. Having lived here for four years, he knows their faces; he continues down the aisle at a speed that is not brusque but implies he isn't at liberty to stop for a chat. He nonchalantly plucks items from the shelves, pretends to study yoghurt brands. In the check-out line, he refrains from being obviously grossed-out by the grease in the cashier's long grey hair, though he can't keep himself from inwardly sneering.

At home, he puts the groceries away (check), takes ground meat out of the freezer to thaw (check), closes the drapes on the side of the house where the afternoon sun will soon make it unbearable (check) and goes to scrub the bathroom sink.

An idea hits him: he decides to do the whole bathroom. Vinegar wipes lime scale from the tiles and removes the dirty yellow tint from the corner behind the door. A speck of hopeful black mould in the edge of the window frame fades beneath an old toothbrush dipped in Borax.

Did he clean it properly?

He Googles it, checks WikiHow. No. He forgot to do the walls and ceiling.

Cranking his iPod, he grabs another rag and starts wiping. Halfway through the ceiling, his arms are beginning to ache. He adopts a pattern—left and right—stretching all his muscles to their limits. Cleaning the walls becomes a thigh-burning dance.

When he's finished, he stands in the bathroom doorway to survey his work. The chrome flashes; the tiles gleam. It looks like something from an ad.

After a lunch that includes all four food groups, he spices the thawed meat for burgers and chops vegetables for a salad. Dishes in the dishwasher. Counters wiped. Floor swept.

His room: he surveys the disaster zone. It's pretty rough, he has to admit.

His eye catches movement outside the window.

They were in the backyard today, back from their vacation. They were just playing. Towel capes tied around their shoulders. They chased imaginary bad guys around the tree trunks, up into the wooden fort. The clashing cardboard swords made a dull slap that I could only hear if I held my breath. Their long, thin, blonde hair flew when they ran, when they swung their weapons at the monsters.

"I killed it!"

"Behind you!"

They attacked things and defended territory for over half an hour until Mrs. Cameron called them in for a snack. They whined about having to go in.

I watched her the whole time. I didn't move from the window once. I didn't even fucking think about moving.

How many goddamned times have I watched her play, not thinking about anything else, not saying anything?

And not telling anyone that I watched her play?

My head is pounding.

There. Took an Ativan. It'll all go away in a bit. Again.

I can't let Mom and Dad find out that I skipped the camp interviews. I'll get in so much shit, and they'll ask so many questions that I won't be able to answer, and I'll just sit there like the dumb fuck that I am.

He slides his journal back inside an old school binder of random papers and shoves the binder to the back of his closet.

When his father comes home, Karl flies down the stairs to meet him. They barbecue the burgers and eat dinner in front of a recorded soccer game. During an intense play, Karl's father is leaning forward and hissing epithets.

"Dad, not only are you yelling at a machine, you're yelling at a machine that's playing a game from two days ago."

"It's instinct. *Mea culpa.* Besides, I believe I heard a 'Messi, whoa!' out of your mouth not five minutes ago."

"Praise is always appreciated. I was being a good person. You didn't hear anything scatological out of *my* mouth, did you? No. That's because you raised me right. What happened to you? Were you raised in a barn?"

"Just be quiet and watch the game, or you'll find yourself scrubbing the toilet."

Karl slouches further down on the sofa. "Been there, done that already today."

Before the sun goes down, Karl gets his father to show him how to scrape the garage door for painting.

Wednesday

Karl and his mother repeat the scene of the previous day. The *deja vu* makes him feel like he has everything under control.

She's rebuttoning the last two buttons of her blouse and tucking it into the neat waistband of her skirt. "I was pleasantly shocked yesterday. Not expecting that again, but I've left another list on the table—just in case it's another day for miracles."

"I think my rosary is somewhere in my room. Shall see which saint can whip something up for you."

"Except you didn't seem to make any plans with friends."

"Meh. Yesterday's saint was a bit of a flake. You get what you pay for."

After hanging a load of laundry on the line, he tackles the garage door while the sun is on the other side of the house. As he did when cleaning the bathroom walls, he pushes his muscles, straining them until they almost screech, gripping the wire brush and the scraper until his finger nails curl around the handle and dig into his palm.

He tests the surface with his eyes closed, feeling for errors, faults. It is smooth. Perfect.

The paint glides on, thick brushstrokes covering the blotchy colours with clean, glossy white. Unsightly grey cracks disappear.

He feels calm on the inside, waiting for the first coat to dry. Lying on the soft grass in the shade of the linden tree, he watches clouds in the topaz-blue sky. His arm muscles slow their burning. For several minutes, he's almost happy.

A burst of energy hits suddenly, unexpectedly. It's too soon to apply the

second coat of paint, so he goes inside to cut
radish roses for dinner and mop the kitchen
floor.

*There's a video on YouTube (no
shit, master of the obvious). The
girl on the video looks a lot like the
girl next door. Her hair is a little
thicker and her eyes aren't as
green, but she reminds me of her.
In the video, she's got her hands
on her hips and she's schooling
her mother in the fine art of
cereal-pouring.*

*I watched that video ten times.
Took another Ativan. It hasn't
kicked in yet. My guts are still
snarled up and my legs are jittery.
I fucking hate this feeling.*

*I don't know why that video came
up in the "suggested for you"
section. What part of my steady
diet of pop music put a little girl
there?*

*Comedy, I guess. Something about
the funny videos I must have
watched.*

Or someone knows. Someone is trying to prove that I can't keep the secret.

But I did so much around the house today that Mom and Dad won't even think about the camp job.

He closes the blinds in his room so he's not distracted by anything. Though his mother was pleased with the state of the room, the closet hasn't been properly cleaned out since he was about twelve. He puts his iPod on the speakers and begins to gut the closet.

His life is in there. On the very top shelf, on the left-hand side, is his baby box. It contains, he knows, the blue bead ID bracelet and miniature white sleepers he wore home from the hospital, his stuffed rabbit that looks like it's decomposing, and his first crayon scribble. His christening dress is on the bottom; the lace is beginning to yellow, despite the white tissue paper.

He dusts the top shelf and returns the box to its corner. He doesn't feel like looking at that stuff now.

The rest of the closet is a mishmash of old school papers and clothes that don't quite fit, birthday gifts that didn't suit him and CDs he hasn't played since his CD player died two years ago. He fills the recycling bin with paper, makes a pile for the blue clothing bin beside the grocery store and fills a small kitchen garbage bag. The closet gets thoroughly vacuumed. Shirts hang to the left, pants to the right; his one sports coat in its plastic cover goes against the wall. The binder that hides his journal gets labelled "Essays and Exams" and is tucked neatly onto the top shelf beside the baby box.

Before he showers, he goes outside to check the garage door. The second coat makes it gleam in purity.

That evening, he realises he has yet to do anything about socialising. He loads the dishwasher and calls out to his parents that he's biking over to the park. He tosses his soccer ball into his backpack, just in case they need extra assurance.

He doesn't stop at the park. There are only little kids and parents there, trying to eke out the last bit of the day. Teenagers don't hang at the park—except for a handful of brown guys playing cricket. The teenagers are at the skate park or under the railway trestle. Karl steers his bike onto the path towards the lakeshore, where he could ride straight for twenty kilometres, if he wanted to. He joins the other cyclists in what's supposed to be the fast lane, but it's too crowded to get up any significant speed.

He lets himself get mixed in with the crowd. No one seems to notice him as anything other than a moving arrangement of simple machinery.

He likes it that way.

Thursday

It is humid and overcast. His mother catches him before he's even out of bed.

"Would you bike over to Grammy's today? She needs these papers that we signed for her. She says she'll feed you lunch, too."

He battles the urge to smash his face back into the pillow. "Sure, no problem. What else should I do today?"

"Cut the grass? Before it rains?"

"Yeppers."

"That means you should probably get up now. It's not looking like it'll hold off for long."

The heaviness of the air seems to be just one more thing to push through. His legs don't want to move; he forces himself down the steps and across the grass to the barn-shaped tool shed. As usual, its metallic, oily smell unsettles him. The shape of the shed makes him expect something more animalistic, more fecund.

He lifts the push-mower from the hooks on the wall, closing his eyes against the rain of dried grass clippings that dislodges from the blades.

In the front yard, he contemplates a new approach to cutting, something other than his usual back-and-forth-whatever. A neat square around the edge of the yard, and a pattern of diagonal stripes to fill the square. His father, en route to the car, gives him a thumbs-up.

The effect is so pleasing that he repeats the pattern in the backyard, getting only momentarily stuck on the awkward corner with the circular herb garden. He settles on a sunburst pattern for that.

From his bedroom window, he surveys his artwork. It's mathematical and almost faultless. Something feels warm and satisfying in his belly.

There's movement in the neighbour's yard: the patio door opens.

He yanks the blinds closed and goes to shower.

I had a dream about Olivia. I haven't thought about her since the day of the camp interviews 4 months ago.

It's funny that the first year at camp, when she was 5 and I was 11, it was okay for us to be together. People called us "friends" and told me how awesome I was, how I was "so good with her". The next year, we sometimes got funny looks from some people. I didn't understand those looks then, but I do now.

Last year, no matter how hard she cried about wanting to be with me, they kept trying to distract her with group activities or treats or even by getting angry with her. It was my fault she kept getting in trouble. When they told me to stay with people in my age group, I know it was because of Olivia. They didn't say anything, but the tone of their voices made my stomach sink.

In the dream I had last night, she just ran past them. We went to play tether ball. I still had to take it easy so she wouldn't lose too badly. She was still young and had her ugly, one-eyed teddy bear with her.

I wonder if she ever wonders why I'm not at camp...

I miss the way she used to choke when we played Sea Monster in the lake because she couldn't stop laughing long enough to blow bubbles. It was contagious. Thinking about it is making me smile now.

He takes an Ativan before he leaves the house.

He's always struck by his grandmother's appearance. Smelling clean like lemon soap, she looks like she's just fallen out of a clothes dryer. Her wild hair and rumpled clothes seem blown in the same direction.

"Oh, good. You're here." She adds the proffered manila envelope to the top of the book pile in her arms. When she leans over to kiss his cheek, the corner of a book pokes his chest and there's the sound of crinkling paper.

"Thank you for bringing this. Come in the kitchen. I'm just clearing the table for lunch."

The table is half-cleared, and the uncluttered half is laid with multicoloured placemats, bright orange plates and blue Mexican glassware. The other half of the table is stacked with papers and books. She adds her armload to this side and turns to the counter.

"Now, do you still eat meat? I know teenagers experiment with social issues. Let

27

me know if you're doing something new. I have no problem accommodating things like that."

He thinks about the way she reacted when his older cousin got a Chinese symbol tattooed on her upper thigh. "Still eating meat, Grammy. All hell hasn't frozen over yet."

She grins at him as she slices slabs from a ham.

"What's in the envelope? What papers did you need Mom and Dad to sign?"

"It's my Living Will. I don't want to end up like those people I saw when I had my surgery in the winter. They're attached to machines and pumped full of chemicals so they can live a few more years lying in bed with nurses wiping their bottoms. That is *not* the way I intend to live. I've spent my whole life trying to be the best at being me, and I will not be reduced to *that* after all my efforts. I don't care what society thinks. They will not take away my right to be human!"

He claps slowly.

"Do not make fun of me, young man." There is a bread knife raised, teeth-first, towards him.

"I'm not. I agree with you. It's an awesome stance to take."

She squints suspiciously. "Good, because that's the stance I'm damned well taking."

As they eat sandwiches and raw vegetables with artichoke dip, she grills him about the marks from his final report card ("All good, Grams. Straight A's except for a B+ in English"), his social life ("They all got jobs this summer") and the video games he's been playing ("Nothing violent except for killing some zombies").

"And what are you doing with your days, dear?"

A sarcastic comment flits through his mind, but he catches himself before it reaches his mouth. "Well, I didn't get the camp job—"

"Yes, your father told me."

"—so I'm helping around the house a lot. I might find a place to volunteer, too."

"Your father also told me you'd been doing that—all the work around the house. He said you'd been amazingly helpful."

"I'm tryin'."

She observes him over the top of her water glass. "Hmm."

"What does *hmm* mean?"

"Nothing. Nothing yet." She continues watching him until he looks away in discomfort. She stands up from the table. "Dessert? It's ice cream."

"Of course."

As they're doing the lunch dishes, she tells him about her therapeutic painting class and all the "beautiful characters" she's met there. He zones out, hands deep in the wash water. There are bubbles popping around his wrists.

It bothers him to put the soapy dishes into the rinse water. Contamination. He wishes he could rinse the dishes under running water and then float them in the clear, hot bath. She'd never allow that, though. Enviro-bunny-hugger. He uses his fingertips to wipe suds from the glass.

"You even listening? You're off in your own world there."

"Yeah. Of course."

"Hmm."

He tries to look innocent—and attentive.

"You could try it some day, the therapeutic painting. There are a couple of young people there. Come with me next week."

"Anyone around the age of fourteen?"

"Well, no, but there's a woman around, I don't know, twenty-five."

"Hmm."

She raises her eyebrows and smiles drily. "I have a couple of chores that would be so much easier with an extra body. Would you help me? It'll just take fifteen minutes or so."

He dries his hands on a purple tea towel. "No problem"

They change a blown lightbulb in the back-hallway ceiling light and hoist a couple of boxes up to the attic.

"Anything else I can do for you?"

She rests her hands on the back of a kitchen chair. "I think I'm okay, thanks."

"You sure? I could vacuum or whatever."

"Karl, is everything okay with you?" She tilts her head in the direction of her hair. "You seem like something might be worrying you."

"Nope." The Ativan suddenly starts wearing off: his stomach begins to clench and there's a headache seeping up his temples.

"Are you thinking you might be gay?"

He coughs out a dry laugh. "No, Grammy. Not gay. I can tell you that."

"Because that's perfectly okay. We don't get to choose who we're attracted to."

"I know it's okay to be gay, but I'm not. Sorry."

"Then what's wrong?"

"Nothing's wrong, Grammy. Absolutely nothing." He kisses her cheek. "I'll go now, if you don't need me. I'm testing out my future as a gourmet chef and making soufflé for dinner."

He pedals through the misty rain, turning his face up to the coolness. There's no breeze; the trees seem to be stretching out to catch the water.

Two blocks from home, he sees flashes of familiar colours in the corner of his eye: yellow rainboots, a bright red raincoat with white trim and brass clasps, and a less-heartwrenching pink one with flowers. He registers the see-through umbrellas waving in the air, swinging in such wide arcs that they could not possibly be protecting anyone from the rain.

Her hair would be damp.

He focuses on the road, blinkering himself with threats and chastisements.

Friday

He gets a haircut. Though he thinks it might make him look like someone who would wear a white shirt and black slacks every day of the week, he asks the barber to cut it very short. He wants to look *clean*, he explains.

In the evening, he takes his bike out. It's easier than crashing in front of the television and having to deal with questions about his social life.

The guys are on the other side of the street. Karl hears Dave bellow at him.

"Carlos, my man!"

"Davos!"

They wave him over. Karl clasps hands with Ari.

Dave pulls him into an all-encompassing hug. "Watch out for pedo-bear!"

"We're the same age, asshole." Karl dismissively pats his shoulder. "You can't be a pedo if we're the same age. You're just a garden-variety faggot."

"Tsk-tsk. You can't use that derogatory term anymore, sir. This is the 21st century—and, besides, I'm not a faggot. I'm an equal-opportunity fucker. If you're naked, I'll fuck you."

"How very millennial of you."

Ari taps the cool metal of Karl's handlebars. "We're meeting Danny and Ethan at the trestle. Wanna come?"

The guys don't have their bikes, which means they got their hands on some beer or something and don't want to get slammed with impaired driving as well as under-age drinking. Karl pretends to mull it over, stroking a non-existent beard on his chin. "Nah, can't. Gotta go do chores. The units are none too pleased about my lack of employment so they're punishing me for the local economy."

Ari grabs hold of both handlebars, straddles the front wheel and rolls Karl back and forth a few centimetres. "Thought you said you were a shoo-in for that camp."

"Guess I was wrong, then."

"Ethan went for it, too. He said he didn't see you there." Dave also grabs a handle bar and starts tilting the bike sideways as Ari pushes and pulls at the front. Karl loosens his muscles to keep his balance.

"It wasn't a long interview. I didn't feel any need to stay there all day."

"Whatever. You should put your name in to volunteer at the food bank with me."

"Doing what?"

"Mostly, I clean the bathrooms and lift boxes—all the shit the seniors don't want to do."

Karl grins at Dave. "Better than cleaning and lifting at home. I'll give it a shot."

"You should come hang this weekend," Ari puts in. "Or go online tonight. We haven't massacred any villains in a while."

"Not tonight. Maybe tomorrow."

"'Kay. Probably won't be in good shape tonight anyway." Ari gestures to Dave's backpack while Dave does a Groucho Marx impression. "Might end up shooting you or something."

"Text me tomorrow when you recover."

"See ya, pedo."

"See ya, faggot."

Karl clasps their hands again and rides off.

He's a little annoyed with his own lack of forethought. Now he has to go home and deal with his parents so no one else sees him riding around town.

At home, his parents are cuddled together on the couch in front of Netflix. They seem a little disappointed that he's home so early, so he tries to accommodate.

"That's freakin' gross. Get a room."

"We have one," his father growls. "We have this room."

"Fine. I'm going to waste the prime of my life playing video games."

"You do that, son."

Saturday

It's dark and silent when he wakes up. His brain tries to dog-paddle through the layers of dream, flails around to grasp reality.

The crotch of his pyjama bottoms is damp, and he suddenly remembers what he dreamed about. He notices his hands are still cupped over his wet groin. Their position is not stimulating: they are protecting.

Nausea rises as his heart sinks. Trying not to think, he gets out of bed to put on clean pyjama bottoms and use the toilet in case one of his parents heard him get up.

Back in bed, he can't focus on reading so he grabs his tablet. Social media is sleeping. None of his YouTubers has posted anything new. He streams a sitcom rerun but can't pay attention to it.

He thinks about pretending to sleep in, but the walls seem too close, the ceiling vertiginously high. At daybreak, he leaps out of bed and into the shower. By the time his parents get up, the clean laundry is hanging on the line, and there are pancakes and fruit salad with yoghurt for breakfast. The extra dose of Ativan makes the sun seem less bright, so he has a brief argument with his mother about the positioning of the kitchen blinds.

"You coming shopping for the new chair?" His mother stands in the doorway, watching him clean up from breakfast. She's wearing a colourless summer dressing gown and yesterday's eye make-up is smeared.

"Got anything that needs doing around here?"

"No, you've done pretty much everything. The house hasn't looked this good since the day before you were born."

He can hear the edge of suspicion creeping behind her voice. "I was thinking of volunteering at the food bank. Dave says it's a good place."

"Fine idea. Why don't you email them while Dad and I get ready? Then we'll do a little family bonding."

"While shopping. Such fun."

"Yes, it will be."

The furniture store is seemingly endless, with spotlights bouncing off bits of chrome and glass, and baskets on every surface. On the way to the back, Karl stops in his tracks to stare at a red bowl-shaped basket filled with sparkly fake grapefruit and kiwi fruit. The basket is on a purple throw blanket on a white leather sofa.

He doesn't know what to think about it.

His mother is beside him, talking in a low voice. "Did you have to take a pill today? You seem a little stoned."

He shakes his head briskly. "I'm good."

He follows her to the discount section at the back and shows an interest in colours and styles, debates the potential longevity of each piece. Will it suit their lifestyle now, he asks them, as well as the empty nest that will be coming up before they know it?

With whinging arms, he helps his dad load the chair into the back of the minivan and tie the hatch lid down. He tries to focus on how they will get the chair installed in the living room and counts down to when he can retreat to his room.

That evening, they attend a barbecue with some family friends. Karl is careful to tuck an extra Ativan into his pocket and bring his tablet so he doesn't get roped into playing with little kids all evening.

Sunday

In trousers that make his thighs sweat so much they feel slimy, Karl sits through the Sunday service. Long ago, he picked up the stand-sit-kneel-sit-stand rhythm, and he's able to zone out for everything except the hand-shaking and Communion.

Sometime during a hymn he is mouthing, it occurs to him what would happen if these people knew about what went on in his head.

He slips another Ativan from his pocket and fakes a sneeze so he can get it in his mouth.

By 1:30, when he drags himself through their front door, the drugs make him fall asleep on the couch. He wakes several hours later, overheated despite the air conditioning. Someone has put a light blanket over him. He makes sure he's alone in the room before checking beneath the blanket. It's only sweat. There was nothing sexual about that dream. Her face was beautiful, but it was terrified.

The fuck? Seven billion people in the world, and God chooses me to be the goddamned pedo.

Monday

There's nowhere to safely burn his journal without setting off the fire alarm or having one of the neighbours ask what he's up to. He resorts to using the other elements to destroy the evidence: he soaks the notebook in the kitchen sink, mashing the wet paper into an amoebic blob and crushing it between the hard covers. In the back yard, crouching between the fence and the sunflowers, he digs a large hole with a garden trowel and lays the notebook to rest a metre below the surface.

MAP Chat: Causes

NotHumbert: Whos that guy that studied us?

PedoProud: German or Canadian?

NotHumbert: Either

PedoProud: Beier, Seto and Cantor.

There are others, too. We're becoming the cool kids now.

The Brits are beginning to like us.

NotYourMother: No one studies us

Not anticontacts

Only offenders

NotHumbert: You know what I mean

Ill take anything going

NotYourMother: Not me

We're different animals altogether

Oskar: Why do you ask, Not Humbert?

NotHumbert: Just in one of those moods where I care about why Im a MAP

NotYourMother: They hypothesize it has something to do with the white matter in our brains

bunnyboy: whats wrong with my white matter

PedoProud: Possibly nothing, @bunnyboy. They've only studied sexual offenders. They don't care about minor attraction as an orientation unless the person has committed a crime. Well, I guess they kind of do, but getting the funding to study us is more difficult.

NotHumbert: I just wish i knew what caused my minor attraction

PedoProud: Me too. It would be worth coming out to the scientists if they could give me some answers—and not report me.

Oskar: In your case, Not Humbert, it is your gender dysphoria that is the cause. Abuse will also cause it.

NotHumbert: ...

PedoProud: I'm speechless.

NotHumbert: I'm not

But I cant talk like that here.

bunnyboy: i wasnt abused and im not trans

NotYourMother: Try to explain as calmly as possible @NotHumbert

Educate whenever possible

NotHumbert: Whole lotta nope

Too freaking pissed

bunnyboy: why would being trans cause anything

why would being abused cause anything

PedoProud: Exactly, @bunnyboy. Being transgender causes being transgender.

That's all.

DontGimmeLolita: Sorry I'm late

kid puked.

Just catching up on reading

wow shoulda come sooner!

bunnyboy: i want to know why im a pedo

no one fucked with me

@NotYourMother its a verb not a swear word

NotYourMother: @bunnyboy a fine verb

DontGimmeLolita: I wasnt date raped until I was 17.

i knew I was a pedo before I was 12

i was definitely born this way

PedoProud: I was abused, but I can't see how that would relate to me being attracted to someone younger.

NotYourMother: @Oskar explain your theories?

Oskar: Most of us were abused. We learned from our abuse.

NotYourMother: @Oskar and the gender dysphoria theory

Oskar: If one cannot choose a gender, one cannot choose an age of attraction.

NotHumbert: I GODDAMNED WELL DIDNT CHOOSE EITHER

PedoProud: Well said, @NotHumbert.

NotYourMother: Keep calm

Getting angry doesnt help

Explaining will

Asking questions will

DontGimmeLolita: @Oskar u said most of us were abused

Only u and @PedoProud were abused as kids

NotHumbert: Okay, i have a question for @Oskar

Do you think all trans people are pedos?

Oskar: I believe the homosexual community has more pedophiles than the heterosexual community does.

NotHumbert: trans ≠ homosexual

Oskar: I am homosexual.

NotHumbert: Im not

Oksar: You are not now. You were when you were a woman.

NotYourMother: Would anyone like to ask a question

bunnyboy: why are u guys so uptight

jokes anyone?

DontGimmeLolita: I got one.

a question not a joke

If we had scientist who could test us without reporting us or having anyone out us, who would want them to try to find out what causes pedophilia

PedoProud: I would.

NotHumbert: Me.

bunnyboy: me

NotYourMother: Me

PedoProud: @NotYourMother, were you abused?

NotYourMother: No

>   At least not by an adult

>   We were the same age and i was an older teenager

>   No obvious reason for me

DontGimmeLolita: Me neither

>   i have no reason

>   Ain't got none at all

PedoProud: Lol!

DontGimmeLolita: Honey i got everything else

>   I dont need no freakin' reason.

>   Besides i'm all about who I am now

about what i do now.

doesnt matter what happened years
ago or 5 minutes ago. Now is now

Rayanna

Rayanna is dreaming. She's on an island with no grownups. Through dusty glasses—though in real life she doesn't wear glasses—she can see bright fruit on rich green trees, and the endless blue of sky and sea. In the distance, she can hear an airplane engine, though she's more concerned about a surmounting heaviness, an ambiguous threat of pain, behind her. She's unsure whether she wants the airplane or the heaviness to reach her first.

When she wakes in her dark room, she chides herself for the dream: there are no lush, adult-free islands on Earth. There is the rest of the novel to read, however, as illness is never an excuse for falling behind in schoolwork. There will be an essay on *Lord of the Flies* when she gets back to school.

Blinking, she stretches cautiously. She's not tired anymore: the fever was mild, but it was enough to make her sleep a lot over the three days. Now that the fever has broken, she feels calm, balanced, good. The hours spent alone have left her with an uncommon amount of energy. Her mind flits from one thought to the next, excited to have such agility again. She notices the texture of the cotton sheets against her hand, a strand of hair that tickles close to her mouth, the glint of the polished brass handles against the dark wood of her dresser.

The house is quiet, and there's no light coming through the cracks around her bedroom door. Her parents must be asleep. Outside her bedroom window, the warm night is black but still occasionally noisy with a passing car or distant teenagers, and what sounds like a racoon excavating a metal garbage can.

The sound briefly breaks through the stream of thoughts in her head. No one on the cul-de-sac has metal garbage cans anymore. That's the sort of thing the neighbourhood committee would have banned a long time ago. They have rules about how things should look and sound. There will be complaints tomorrow: neighbours snarking to each other and sending emails to the appropriate people. By noon, the offending resident will be well-aware of their sin.

She yawns. Her tablet is on her bedside table. She props herself up against the headboard and turns the tablet on so she can finish reading *Lord of the Flies*. If she's at all well, she'll be sent back to school tomorrow. Her father doesn't approve of molly-coddling.

The screen clicks on smoothly, cleanly, with all the apps in their assigned places. There's a pleasure to be found in the order, in the intense colours of the screen. Her clean, stub-nailed finger hovers over the book app but doesn't tap it. A thought flickers through her brain. The dream. The thing she discovered the other night.

She repositions the tablet more squarely on her lap.

The tablet stares at her as though it can hear her heart thudding. Deliberately refraining from thinking, she quickly goes into the settings and over-rides the parental controls her father put on the tablet.

She taps the keypad: *p e d*—and then erases it. Her heart races, and she berates her own stupidity.

She opens an incognito window.

p e d o p h i l e

The results slot themselves into place, just like they did a month ago.

The top-story news articles use words she expects: "violent pedophile hid so he could rape her"; "I want that sick madman punished!"; "pedo-lover hypocrite"; "pedophile ring shut down".

There are images of ugly, weird old men.

The rest of the links still seem scientific, academic.

Only part of the internet is actively out to get her.

Her heart rate slows a little. Though the results are the same as they were two weeks ago when she first did a search, she is again surprised by the neutrality of the links she taps on.

Squinting against the brightness of the screen, she reads the Wikipedia page, soothed by its familiar format. The first part is hard to read, with medical language and long sentences. Further down, it gets easier—easier to read, to understand.

It gets easier to breathe.

She hasn't *chosen* this, it says. She has just *discovered* it.

Yes. She knows that.

She breathes again and looks up at the wall opposite her, where a streetlight has splayed a triangle of white light. Taylor Swift gazes down from the poster that's been up for more than three years. She should replace it, she thinks. That poster has seen a lot, and she doesn't hear Taylor Swift much anymore. At school, which is the only place she can listen to music, the kids are now into darker, heavier music which suits her even better. Where Taylor wrote songs Rayanna understood and enjoyed, the new music seeps into her psyche, swirls through her brain and sweeps up intense energy hidden in nooks and crannies.

But maybe she would miss Taylor. Her maternal grandfather had given her the poster, saying it was good for Rayanna to have modern role models to look up to. Between the music and the poster, Taylor became a large part of Rayanna's days for quite some time.

The poster was the first thing her mother had ever defended from Rayanna's father.

There's a sound from somewhere in the house. With rehearsed speed, she flicks off the tablet and shoves it beneath the head of her mattress. In the darkness, she feigns sleep for a good ten minutes before she's sure it's safe again.

Back on Google, she finds WikiHow's "How to Identify a Pedophile". Part of her wants to laugh. Another part of her shudders and squirms, but she reads the article. Again, it's sensible. Pedophiles aren't formed in a mould.

She imagines putting her photo in there.

She hits the *back* button.

The last time she looked at this, there was something intriguing at the bottom of the first page, in the related searches. It was a man's name. A real pedophile? The name is still there. She taps it. There's an article about him, about how he's a "virped". She doesn't understand what that means, but the article isn't hate-filled so it must be okay.

He's on Twitter. He's real; he has a real photograph, one that looks like a normal man without the eerie leer of the pedophiles in the news articles. She reads and taps some more.

There are quite a few of them on Twitter. Some argue with each other: there are words she doesn't quite understand in that context—*pro* and *anti*—and accusations of sex with kids. Three of them are getting death threats, but they don't seem to be taking them very seriously.

Some are discussing pedophilia, and some are making jokes.

They make jokes about pedophilia, and they are pedophiles.

They have names—realistic names like *Luke* and *Andrew*, but she starts to think they might be pseudonyms. There are others with more normal user names, things that are clearly made-up. Only the one guy seems to have a real photograph: the rest hide behind illustrated images of people. There are a few dogs, cats and flowers, but mostly anime characters.

One uses a picture of an island in a blue sea.

Rayanna smiles to herself as the origins of her dream click into place, and she marvels at the bravery of these Twitter pedophiles.

She reads their Twitter timelines for more than half an hour. The more she taps, the more she finds. There are hundreds of them, all talking about people like her.

A heavy wave of emotion brings tears to her eyes, and her head feels as though her fever has returned. After carefully checking to make sure the browsing history is clear and resetting the parental controls, she shuts off the tablet and lies back against the pillows.

It's several hours before she falls back into a dream-heavy sleep.

The next morning, awake and dressed for school, she's pleasantly surprised to see a white pill in her father's hand, instead of a blue one. She'd forgotten how much time had passed. Bowing her head a little so her long hair hides her expression, she accepts the pill and the tumbler of water he holds out to her.

Her period will start later this evening or early tomorrow morning: her father won't touch her for a week.

The combination of illness and her period will give her more time alone than she's had in a long while. The thought sends a stream of warmth through her upper chest. She flings her backpack over her left shoulder and goes to wait in the back seat of the car.

The pedophiles are still in her head. Over the course of the night, while she was sleeping, they've assembled themselves into a little community in the back of her mind, waiting for her to return and read what they've written. Or maybe they're writing now, as she walks into the school. Who are they talking to—who are they educating and who are they ignoring? She imagines herself as one of them, coolly discussing the science behind her sexual attraction even as trolls spew insults and threats at her. They wouldn't be able to touch her; she is protected by facts and a symbolic profile image.

By second-period geography class, she is sufficiently distracted to earn a curious look from her teacher.

"Are you feeling all right, Rayanna?"

She scrambles to excuse the rare inattention. "I think I just need a drink of water?" She pretends to absent-mindedly rub her temples.

"Of course."

The lid to her metal water bottle clinks as she opens it. The teacher returns to the lesson.

For the rest of the day, Rayanna digs her thumbnail into her index fingertip every time her mind threatens to go off-track.

It's not until about 3:30, after she has been driven home from school and eaten the snack her mother put in front of her, that she loosens the reins. Her textbooks are spread on the desk in front of her, but her mind is flipping through memories of her classmates' manga: images of attractive girls with blonde pigtails, short school-girl skirts over slender legs, a hint of cleavage at the necklines of their blouses. None of them seem right. They are not her. Even on Twitter, she couldn't be a cute, blonde schoolgirl.

She dredges up the ebony-haired ones with huge, impossible curves. No. Definitely not something like that.

Then she remembers a TV show someone had been watching on their phone during lunch. A not-too-pretty girl with awkward angles and wild pink hair.

Yes. That one. That anime girl is the one she wants to be.

That one is the one she wants to represent her forever.

That night, her mother brings a hot water bottle for the cramps, though Rayanna doesn't really need it. She never really needs it; she likes the excuse to spend a couple of minutes alone with her mother, taking up all the attention. She likes her mother lightly rubbing her back through the blankets, stroking her hair. They usually don't speak. The silence is relaxing, and she also doesn't have to worry about her father eavesdropping.

Her mother's hand smooths circles over the small of Rayanna's back. As Rayanna lies on her side, her mind drifts.

A name. She needs a name to go with the wild pink girl. Nothing feminine like her own.

Her mother's name—no, that might be traced back to her. Not *Taylor*, because sharing something like this with such a normal woman would be wrong.

She curls herself tighter around the hot water bottle. Her mother rubs a little harder and coos sympathetically.

"Mama?"

Her mother blinks. "Yes, sweetie?"

"How did you choose my name?"

"Your father chose it."

"Why did he choose *Rayanna*?"

"I didn't ask him, of course. It seemed to suit you: beautiful and sweet."

Rayanna leans back against her mother's hand. "What would you have chosen for me?"

"Oh, I can't think about that now. *Rayanna* is who you are. You're too old for me to think up new names for you."

She glances up at Taylor Swift. "How about *Taylor*?"

Her mother smiles weakly. "I think *Rayanna* is better."

"What if I didn't want to be Rayanna anymore? Lots of people change their names."

"Those people are hiding something. We are who we are. We cannot change what God has made of us."

Frustration zips through her, but she thinks trying to reason with her mother might be even more irritating.

Her mother reaches up to smooth Rayanna's hair from her forehead. "Is that better?"

"It's good. Thank you, Mama."

"Sleep well, sweetheart." Before leaving the room, she cracks the window for fresh air—the five centimetres the safety locks permit.

In the darkness, with the neighbourhood noise wafting through the window, Rayanna moves the water bottle up and cuddles it like a teddy bear.

The pink-haired girl's name will not be *Rayanna*—nor *Taylor*, as that is a cute blonde girl's name that evokes a confident sassiness.

Outside, the boys are yelling obscenities. "Fucking bitch cunt!"

She won't be any of those either. Not on Twitter.

When the night is quiet, she reaches for her tablet again.

She can read their Tweets, but she can't respond to them until she makes an account with a user name. Her mouse hovers over the button; anxiety churns in her chest.

Instead, she opens YouTube. With the sound off and the subtitles on, she watches a TEDx Talk by a doctor who wants to talk about pedophilia.

Rayanna notes that she's the first kind of pedophile the doctor describes: the kind that wants to look at the department-store magazine of the kids in bathing suits. She's not the kind to look at pictures of naked kids whose faces, she thinks, would be the sad kind that her father tells her to wipe off. She's not the kind who would ever touch a kid, even once.

She's certainly not the kind who would do it over and over and over, feeding her child birth control pills so there would be no consequences.

The video finishes. She lies still, staring blankly at the YouTube recommendations.

She likes being the first kind—the kind "over here, on this end of the spectrum". She's proud to not be the other kind on the other end of the spectrum. That kind deserves any punishment that any god could conjure.

Though the water bottle is still a little too hot, she yanks the floral hand-towel off it and holds the hot rubber against her chest.

The teacher's announcement of "groupwork time" makes Rayanna's stomach sink. The other two girls already have their desks together; Rayanna scrapes hers over the linoleum until it butts up against theirs.

Their faces are blank. She understands the dichotomy: her company is not at all pleasurable, but the embarrassment of being forced to work with her is worth the good marks they'll get—and they know Rayanna will do any work they don't feel like doing.

"Hey, Ray."

"Hey."

Rayanna knows their names—Sarah and Kylie—but sometimes has difficulty telling them apart: light brown hair cut just above their breasts and parted in the middle, hazel eyes grudgingly enhanced by nothing more than clear mascara, and pink-tinted lip balm in accordance with the school dress code. Their school uniforms serve only to enhance their similarities.

They begin to whine about the assignment. "I don't know why we have to do this. It's a boys' book. They should let us read something that's about women. We've had enough books about white men. This English class makes it seem like Feminism never happened."

"I know, right? It's unconstitutional. We should complain."

Rayanna is already drawing ruler lines on a piece of paper, entitling the page *Identity and Archetypes in William Golding's **Lord of the Flies***. Down the left-hand side, she lists the major characters, and she starts writing their archetypal roles in the middle column.

With the authority of a military salute, Sarah/Kylie jams her hand into the air. The teacher walks over.

"Yes, girls?"

"We object to the sexism of this book. We think we should read something that's more gender-diverse. This book isn't appropriate for modern society. It encourages the idea that men are the only ones who can organise a civilisation."

The teacher surveys them for a few seconds; Rayanna pauses her writing.

"Do all of you agree?"

"Yeah, of course." Sarah/Kylie looks at Rayanna. "Ray, you agree with me and Sarah."

Rayanna swallows, though her mouth is dry. "There are a lot of boys in this book, yeah."

The teacher is reading Rayanna's chart over her shoulder. She taps a blood-red fingernail on one of the squares Rayanna has filled in. "I think you should talk about this some more, girls, amongst yourselves. Rayanna has an idea that might help you deal with part of this problem. It doesn't address your concerns entirely—in fact, it supports them—but it might be a place to start." She smiles directly at Rayanna. "I do agree with you, though. The curriculum isn't keeping up with the times." She walks away.

Kylie looks at Rayanna. "Whatcha got, Ray?"

Rayanna pushes the chart towards them. "Piggy is a maternal archetype. He's kinda like a wannabe feminist, too."

Sarah snorts. "Bullshit. A guy's a guy. He can't change who he is. That's English-teacher bullshit." She sticks her hand up in the air again.

Rayanna smiles a little, but she's taken aback by the scatological vocabulary, and the fact that her mother and Sarah think the same way.

When the teacher returns, Sarah rephrases her comment using the word *garbage*.

"Fair enough," the teacher concedes. "Perhaps you could look at it a different way, then. Rather than saying Piggy *is* a woman, maybe you could discuss it as a single dominant aspect of the character. Is it a mask or a defense mechanism?"

Kylie raises her hand, even though the teacher is right beside her. "It's a mask."

"To hide what? What would femininity hide when one is stranded on an island with only boys?"

There's a short silence before Sarah speaks. "It's gotta be a mask. Being a girl on the island wouldn't be beneficial to him, but a feminine mask would hide his failure at being a real guy."

Rayanna is surprised that she and Sarah could think the same thing.

The teacher taps the edge of Rayanna's desk again. "Good start, girls. Keep going."

"That's pretty lame," Kylie quips. "Failing at being a guy."

The words bolt from Rayanna's mouth without permission. "Maybe he was too embarrassed to share."

"What'zat?"

"Maybe whatever makes him feel masculine is something the other guys would think is bad." She speaks to the chart in front of her. "Maybe what might make him masculine is something the other guys would hate him for."

Sarah sneers a little, grabs the chart from under Rayanna's hands and starts writing. "Let's just do what the teacher says. Failure at being a real man...."

Kylie purses her glistening lips. "They're all failures. A bunch of women wouldn't start treating each other like animals."

Her father comes to her room a night earlier than she expected, a towel in his hand. She's relieved she still hasn't thought of a name, so she isn't online. It is, for the first time, difficult to hide her impatience, waiting for him to finish sweating and grunting, to leave her alone.

She's been thinking about the online people. She wants to see what Luke and the others are saying to the trolls tonight—though it's usually the same thing, she's noticed: unchosen condition; attraction, not molestation; children can never consent. There are two varieties of trolls they have to deal with: the pedo-hunters and the pedophiles who say children can consent. Rayanna feels a thrill when Luke insults the latter. He uses words on them that he doesn't use on anyone else. His vitriol is vicious and quick, whipping their evil ideas from his timeline, leaving nothing but smoking corpses and a display of his weapons. Despite his cute manga avatar, Rayanna thinks of Luke as a man in medieval armour, sitting astride a horse. Like King Arthur or someone. Turning her face into the pillow so her father can't see, she smiles at her own ridiculous romantic notions.

When her father finally leaves, Rayanna cleans herself up, still thinking about shining armour. As she stands in the cold, sterile bathroom, rinsing the bloodstain from the towel, the name comes to her: *Lancelot*.

She can be the one to wear the armour.

When both the house and outside neighbourhood are silent with sleep, she photoshops a silver helmet on the wild girl, leaving a tuft of pink hair sticking out on either side.

She makes a secret email account that her father probably won't be able to trace.

She creates the Twitter account, uploading her helmeted image and cautiously typing the name *Pink Lancelot*.

Her bio is copied from the other guys': *anti-contact MAP*. As an afterthought, she adds *wild warrior*. Who knows, she thinks. Maybe she'll get braver as she gets older.

It's 3:30 a.m. She needs to sleep but knows she won't.

She follows them—all of them, anyone with the word *anti-contact pedophile* or *MAP* in their bio. There are a lot of them.

Within a couple of hours, they've all followed her back.

"Welcome to Twitter @pinklancelot. Nice to meet u."

MAP Chat: Coming Out

bunnyboy: found a good joke

what should u do if ur afraid of pedophiles

NotHumbert: Grow up.

Heard that one before.

PedoProud: Ha! That's a good one!

DontGimmeLolita: Wouldnt save u from the likes of me

Bwahaha!!!!!

PedoProud: Where did you hear that one, @bunnyboy?

bunnyboy: website

PedoProud: @Oskar, you're quiet.

Do you object to the joke?

Oskar: No. I am still laughing.

I am laughing too hard.

The play on words.

I must excuse myself to get a glass of water.

NotYourMother: Why do you like that joke @bunnyboy

bunnyboy: just strikes me as funny

> i think im exclusive like @Oskar

DontGimmeLolita: What makes u say that

bunnyboy: new kid in school

> everyone says hes hot

> even the guys

> his muscles are too big

Oskar: That was how I was made aware of my attraction, too.

NotHumbert: Oh yeah. You two are both BL.

Oskar: Yes. By the time I was the age of Bunny Boy, I had to admit I would not be attracted to adults.

DontGimmeLolita: Must be frustrating

> And lonely

PedoProud: I once overheard someone—a total stranger in a coffee shop—telling a story about a friend.

> The friend apparently looked very young, even though she was an adult.

The one-night-stand was clearly a MAP, the woman said, based on what he wanted her friend to do in bed. Of course, she didn't use the term "MAP".

I keep wondering how he'll find what he needs.

NotHumbert: He should have told her before they hooked up

PedoProud: Would you tell a hook-up you're a pedo?

NotHumbert: Good point

But I wouldn't try to use someone like that without telling them.

DontGimmeLolita: Hard on the guy though

PedoProud: I know, right?

It was really hard to keep my mouth shut. I wanted to defend him.

NotYourMother: @bunnyboy How are you feeling about being exclusive

bunnyboy: meh

its okay

ill live

Oskar: Yes. You will live.

Paul

It's Paul's favourite time of day. He thinks of it as a transformation zone, like in Superman stories. He's put a frozen meat pie in the oven, made a green salad, and opened a bottle of red so it can breathe. While waiting the last few minutes until her return, he washes the day's dishes.

Katherine's entrance is predicable cacophony: the slamming door, the keys ringing into the glass bowl, the thud of her briefcase on the wooden floor just beyond the foyer. Her stilettoes are also part of the pattern, clicking on the terracotta tiles, then a *shwoop*, *shwoop*, as she yanks them off her feet, and a final double *clunk* as she drops them on the rubber mat.

"Hey!"

She calls back amidst the swoosh of coat and silk scarf. "Hey, yourself! I'm home!"

"I noticed."

Rarely does he spend time with Katherine: by the time she arrives in the kitchen, she's well on her way to being Kate again. Though she's still wearing a suit and nylon stockings when she kisses him, her hands are in the process of pulling the fastener from her bun and letting her light brown hair fall past her shoulders.

"How was work, sweetie?"

"Good." Paul pours wine for both of them and holds her glass out to her. "Fired that one cunt of a client and picked up two more projects. One of them's pretty big. It might turn into something regular, too."

"You gonna take the cunt to court?"

"Nah. I got most of the money he owes. He can try whatever smear campaign he likes. My reviews are great, and his are total shit."

"Why'd you take him, then?"

"We gotta eat, babe."

Kate's snort offends him. She doesn't need to voice the fact that her income is twice his.

He moves her wine glass away from her a little. "Go change. Dinner's almost ready."

He fills a plate for both of them and carries the food into the living room. After finding the remote (with the bonus of finding it before she notices he'd misplaced it again), he flicks on the wide-screen over the fireplace.

Kate returns wearing soft blue jeans and a light pink t-shirt, with her hair in braids, no make-up: his favourite outfit.

She looks at the plate on the coffee table and freezes. "You're fucking kidding. We've been through this."

"It's fine. There's no one here to see. Just eat it."

"I don't want *you* to see spinach stuck in my braces, either."

"It doesn't bother me." With a stockinged foot, he pushes the plate closer to her. "It's kinda cute."

"Salad stuck in braces isn't cute. It's disgusting."

"Nah, you look like a kid. Goes well with the outfit."

She glares at him but picks up the plate.

"That reminds me," he says by way of distraction. "We got one last RSVP. Your mother's high-school teacher? I called the caterer and the hall, so it's all settled."

"Oh my god. I thought we were free and clear. Who rizvips two days before a wedding?"

"Judging by the responses I got from the caterer and the hall, at least one for every wedding. The better question would be, 'Who attends their former student's daughter's wedding?'"

Her feet are tucked up against her bottom, and she rests her plate on her knees. Though he has torn the greens into bite-sized pieces, she folds them and stacks them on her fork before ostentatiously delivering them to the very back of her mouth.

"Jesus, Kate."

"You're not the one who looks like a child."

"No one notices clear braces."

"I do."

"You didn't *have* to get them."

"I could have gone into my thirties looking like Gollum."

"I loved you even with crooked teeth. Don't blame me for your perfectionism."

"Piss off, Mr. Perfect, who is self-employed and not battling glass ceilings."

He sighs. "Why are you feeling insecure today?"

Another glare.

"Finish eating and I'll give you a massage. Here. Have some more wine."

They finish eating in silence, watching a sitcom on T.V. When she clunks her plate onto the coffee table and drains her glass, he pulls her onto his lap.

"Bad day?"

She wraps an arm around his neck and lays her head on his shoulder. "No, not really. Just stressed about getting everything ready for Saturday."

"It doesn't have to be perfect, you know." He rocks her a little. "It might be 'our special day' but it can still have things that don't go as planned."

"I want it perfect. I don't want to trip going up the aisle or something."

"Then you shoulda bought different shoes. Those things are lethal."

"You said you wouldn't snoop!"

"You booby-trapped the dress bag with that single hair in the zipper, but you left the shoe box right where I could see it."

"Cheat."

"You said nothing about shoes." He strokes her bare arm, going under the sleeve to the top of her shoulder. "We have all day tomorrow to finish up the preparations. What still needs doing?"

"Not much, actually. Just confirming the deliveries. Rehearsal's at five, dinner's at seven. We're spending most of the day at the spa."

"Wyatt's flight gets in at eleven. We can check on the deliveries. Just make sure I've got the whole list."

Kate turns her chest against his so he can rub her back. He slips his hand under her shirt to run his fingers along the knobs at the top of her spine, feel the smooth skin of the small of her back. Her hair is silky against his lips. When he moves his hand down, he marvels again at the way it covers most of her thigh.

She playfully shoves his shoulder. "Uh-uh. A whole week. Wedding night. We agreed."

He groans. "Revirgination isn't a thing."

"Delayed gratification is."

"I might die by Saturday night."

"Then you'd miss the surprise."

"What's that?"

"Stay in survival mode for another forty-eight hours and you'll find out."

"Fuuuuuuuuuuuuck."

"On Saturday, yes."

Pretending to massage her upper arms, he runs his thumbs along the simple lines of her tiny, braless breasts. "Fine. I'll be good."

"Can I ask a favour?" She looks intently at his face.

"Yeah."

"Shave for the wedding? Please?"

Another groan. "So much for my masculinity."

His thin beard is roughed up by her fingertips. "Just for the photos."

"That surprise had better be worth it."

On Friday morning, he picks up Wyatt at the terminal and they do a couple of errands. After dumping Wyatt's bags by the pullout couch in Paul's office, they devour the subs they picked up, washing the food down with local micro-brewery beer.

"What's the plan?" Wyatt mumbles around meatballs and bread.

"Not much until the rehearsal dinner."

"Got a theatre that has matinées? I could see that new Star Wars again."

"Yeah, yeah. I haven't seen it yet."

"Not yet? Have you been sick or something?"

Paul clears his throat. "Nah. Kate put a moratorium on movie theatres."

"Why? She freaking about the cost of the wedding? It'll be part of my wedding present to you. Kinda like a really shitty stag party."

"No, no. Different reason."

Wyatt raises an eyebrow.

"I fucked up."

"In a theatre?"

"I bought an adult and a youth ticket, and no one called her out on it."

Wyatt laughs. "Asshole."

Paul twists his mouth. "Slept on the couch for almost a week."

"Did you get to see the movie?"

"Yeah, she didn't find out until we got home and she was throwing out the ticket stub."

"Asshole," Wyatt repeats, grinning.

Though he returns Wyatt's grin, Paul feels a thin stream of the hot humiliation as he remembers Kate's anger. Even when he claimed it was just a joke, meant only to get the annoying teenage ticket seller in trouble, her face had blazed with a fury he'd never seen. He stood in the corner, watching her storm around the bedroom, feeling as though he'd lost control of reality. Thinking about it now, he starts to frown but quickly shakes the feeling off.

"Yeah, we'll go to the theatre on the other side of town."

In grey afternoon light, Paul stands at the front of the church with Wyatt slightly behind him. From the front pew, his mother and father offer him proud, encouraging expressions, just like they used to when he stood on the edge of the pool before a swim meet.

His heart begins to beat a little too quickly. He thinks about the times she's been angry with him, the weirdness that is Katherine in her business suit and make-up. She has a couple of little habits that can sometimes pile up irritation at the back of his neck until he has to leave the room before he slaps her across the face.

He looks over to Wyatt. Wyatt's eyes widen when he sees Paul's expression, but then he levels a calm gaze, and Paul's heart slows. Wyatt claps a hand on Paul's shoulder, and Paul nods imperceptibly.

The organist switches to Pachelbel's *Canon in D Major*; Paul turns to face the back of the nave.

His bride is stunning, heartbreakingly-beautiful. Her dress is a simple Empire cut in plain white silk, and her veil, which frames her face and falls to her elbows, is edged with eyelet. Despite the height of her shoes, she walks steadily towards him. Heat fills his lower belly, and he smiles widely.

This is his wife.

He's barely flipped the lock on the hotel room door when she's got one hand on his chest and the other behind his head, pulling him down so she can kiss him. The soft fabric of her light blue going-away dress slides over her hips, beneath his hands.

He scoops her up, carries her to the bed and begins undressing her. Working around his arms, her hands undo his tie and the buttons on his waistcoat, her tiny fingers slithering between his shirt buttons, each touch of her fingertips on his skin producing a shiver of electricity.

He wants her naked, though he pauses to pay ersatz attention to the expensive padded bra that still only gives her A-cup breasts and the matching panties that skim her public line—and then he notices there is no hair.

"No. Shit...." He grins, trailing a finger along the top of her panties.

"Vanessa convinced me to do it. Happy wedding day."

He looks up. She's reclining on white pillows, her hair spread out around her shoulders. Slowly, he removes her lace bra and pushes her flat on the bed so her breasts almost disappear, then slides the lace underwear down her legs. She is smooth and clean, and everything his body and mind crave.

The following morning, he rests in the stripes of sunlight coming through the vertical blinds. Beside him, she is asleep on her stomach, her lips slightly parted, her hands curled into relaxed fists.

His hand automatically reaches for her, cups over her small bott, but then he catches himself. A show r and a lot of mouthwash are required. His mind shivers as he cleans himself up and quietly brings in the breakfast cart of croissants and mimosas.

He tightens the thick terrycloth bathrobe over his erection and slides back into bed. When he reaches out to stroke her shoulders, she snuggles in, half-awake, her head against his chest. Her hair is messy, a charming echo of innocence.

"You smell all clean," she murmurs to his chest, ending the sentence with a couple of gentle kisses to his sternum.

His cock pulses. "You smell delicious."

"I do not."

"You do." He inhales the baby-powder scent of her deodorant, the fresh-laundry smell that never leaves her. The skin along her spine is smooth; reaching, he moves his hand down until he can touch the silky skin on the inside of her thigh. He closes his eyes, but the thought of her bare body is as obsessively-distracting as the sight of it.

He subtly moves his hips until his erection rubs against something—anything—vaguely solid.

She pats his hip. "My god. We should get married every weekend, if this is what happens." Her teeth nip at the tender skin on his throat, her braces leaving light scratches. "Hold on. I need to pee."

After the toilet flushes, he can hear the water running for a long time. She must be washing her sweet, naked cunt. His lips part as he thinks about it.

When she comes out, yawning loudly, she kneels on the bed and opens his bathrobe. "Well. We can't leave that unattended." With small fingers and a darting tongue, she starts with his balls and works her way up the shaft. Her body curls over his groin, like a child hunched over an interesting toy. He feels like he might explode.

"Let me under you," he gasps, already turning to 69 her. The smell of soap only diminishes the pleasure a little. He comes in a few minutes. She can't take it all; it spills onto his abdomen.

Still breathing heavily, he flips her on her back so he can also use his fingers to bring her to climax. When she settles, he protectively cups his hand over her mons and rests his head on her thigh.

He almost says *I love your cunt* but catches himself in time. "I love you."

"I love you, too, husband. That was a great way to start the marriage." Her fingers nestle in his hair.

He kisses the skin just above her thigh. "Let me have fifteen minutes and some breakfast, and we'll keep this great start going."

Later, as she lowers herself onto his erection, he holds her hips to slow her down, savouring the sight of his cock sinking into her hairless vulva. He raises himself so he can lick her nipples, the backs of his fingers striking the flat lines of her chest. "Oh, god, Katy, my love."

Two weeks later, after a honeymoon spent mostly in bed, the signs of Katherine begin to return.

"You need another waxing."

"No way." She's making weed brownies to satisfy a craving. Her thin arms strain to cream the butter with a fork. "We need to replace that mixer. Here. Smuck this for me." She hands him the bowl and the fork.

"Why not?"

"No, I said we *need* to replace that mixer."

"No, I meant to say, 'Why not wax again?'"

"It fucking hurts, sweetie. That was a one-time, wedding-present thing."

"Oh. What if I shaved again?"

"That was just for the wedding photos." She drops a kiss on his mouth. "I prefer you with a beard. You know that."

He thinks for a minute. "What if you shaved? That doesn't hurt, does it?"

"It's itchy growing back. You try shaving down there."

He imagines it, but the thought of two shaved bodies seems bland, flat. "I'll trim for you."

"You do that anyway."

He hands her the bowl with the softened butter. "I really liked that wedding present." He embraces her from behind, leaning down a little to rest his chin on the top of her head. "Really, really, *really* liked that. C'mon, Katy. Please?"

Her body stiffens. "Why have you started calling me 'Katy' so much?"

"Sorry. I'll stop. Kate."

"Outta my way. I'll let you know when the brownies are done."

They eat the brownies while sitting on the sofa to binge-watch *Being Human*. Kate sits against the arm of the sofa, with a pillow between them. Paul can feel the cold wall.

"I'm sorry I pissed you off."

She speaks to the TV screen. "It's okay."

"Really? You still seem annoyed."

She tosses the pillow on the floor and scoots over to lean her head on his chest. Suddenly, he needs her close: he pulls her onto his lap and clamps her in with both arms, and she tilts her head up for a quick kiss.

That night when they're making love before going to sleep, he avoids looking at her cunt, spending more time on the rest of her body so perhaps she won't notice his lack of interest in going down on her. Though he wasn't aware of it as a problem before the honeymoon, her regrowing pubic hair now disgusts him. He concentrates on the way her small face looks in his large hands, her smooth underarms, her toothpick calves and tiny feet.

When she lowers herself onto him, he can't watch. He shifts his gaze to her breasts, but quickly closes his eyes and remembers the way she looked on their wedding night. Soon, he gets carried away, doesn't notice that, though her body is moving, her facial expression is stony. As he orgasms, he mutters through his teeth. "Good, Katy, that's good. Good girl. Ah, fuck, Katy."

Even before the spasms have completely finished, she pushes away from him, clamping a sheet over the front of her body. He lies on his back, panting, and rests a hand on her sheet-swathed knee.

A whirlwind, she leaps off the bed and flies to the bathroom, slamming the door behind her. He hears the shower running as he drifts off.

The banging of the dresser drawers awakens him. Her wet hair has made damp splotches on the back of her t-shirt, and her feet are bare beneath her jeans. After a couple of minutes, he realises her movements involve putting things into two suitcases.

"Katy?" He sits up and covers his lap with a pillow.

Her eyes are red-rimmed and puffy; her movements are jerky. "What?"

"What are you doing?"

"Leaving you."

For a moment, he's unsure if he heard her correctly, but the words seem to match her actions. "Kate. Stop. Stop." He holds a palm up. "What's going on? I don't understand."

"You're a pedophile. I'm leaving you."

"The fuck? I'm not a pedophile! I'm married to you! You're an adult." He speaks quickly over the rising flush of heat and nausea.

She swipes at a tear. "Did you ever love me, or was it just about me looking young?"

"What are you talking about? I'm no pedo!"

The suitcases slam shut, and she speaks over the violent sound of zippers. "You don't like my work clothes, you get off on passing me off as a twelve-year-old at the movies, and now you want my body shaved like a prepubescent's. You even *call* me by a little girl's name! You are so fucking sick!"

The suitcases thud on the floor.

"You can't even scrape up the goddamned decency to look at me when we fuck. No, don't try to tell me I'm wrong! I watched you! You ignore any part of me that looks remotely adult. You have to close your eyes and pretend I'm some *child*. I knew this would happen! Vanessa said I should wax as a wedding present to you, but I just knew it would feed into your fantasies. That's what really pisses me off: *I knew it*, and I did it anyway. I should have tested you before we went through the whole wedding shit. What a fucking joke! There I was, thinking I was just being oversensitive and that you were a good person. How could I have been so fucking stupid?

"I'm going to Vanessa's. She's picking me up now. I'll text you the name of my lawyer when I get one—and I'll be getting one fucking *first thing* tomorrow morning. You can contact me through them—"

He opens his mouth to protest, but she puts both hands over her ears and continues, her voice rising in pitch.

"This apartment is still in my name, so I want you out of here by the end of the week!"

She raises her voice even more as she heads out the front door. "And you might want to delete whatever kiddie porn or hentai or fucking whatever you have on your computer. If you give me any sort of shit from now until the fucking END OF TIME, I WILL REPORT YOU, YOU SICK FUCK!"

He remains frozen on the bed, listening to the last of the thumping and bumping and slamming, and then the apartment is silent.

He sits on the bed for a long, long time.

MAP Chat: Ticking Time-Bomb Monster

bunnyboy: how do i stop myself

NotHumbert: Stop yourself from what?

bunnyboy: from hurting a kid

NotHumbert: How do you stop yourself from stealing things or killing people?

bunnyboy: thats not the same thing

PedoProud: Yeah, @bunnyboy, it is the same thing.

You don't have to really stop yourself from committing other crimes, do you?

NotHumbert: Do you ever actually feel like you're going to snap and rape someone?

bunnyboy: no

but

NotHumbert: If you don't feel it why worry about it

bunnyboy: cause im a pedo

Oskar: Society has made you worry about something that does not require worry.

96

PedoProud: Are there any signs you might do that, @bunnyboy?

bunnyboy: no

    but what if

DontGimmeLolita: What if what honey?

bunnyboy: what if i kinda like a kid

    i think about how it could happen

PedoProud: Fantasising about a relationship is something everyone does.

    That doesn't mean they'll sexually assault someone.

NotHumbert: I feel like a monster sometimes but I remind myself that I'm not one.

    I've done nothing wrong

Oskar: You are free to think of yourself as a monster. That is the prerogative of every human being. Many people would like you to think of yourself as a monster, but doing so does not help you or protect the children.

DontGimmeLolita: Ur not a monster honey

    if u commit a crime then ur just a criminal.

It aint actually helpful to be afraid of what u are

No matter what the trolls tell u

PedoProud: It won't do anyone any good to think of yourself as a greasy old man who's just a ticking time bomb.

Unless you are that. Some people have sex addictions to add to their orientation.

Oskar: We cannot make society like us, but we do not have to hate ourselves just because they do.

bunnyboy: i hate myself less when im on drugs

PedoProud: Chemical castration?

bunnyboy: weed

Oskar: Then it is an artificial love for yourself.

bunnyboy: hey i never used that word

i said i hate myself less

Oksar: You must learn to love yourself. Humans die if they are unloved. I have lived long enough to see this happen to many people.

NotHumbert: Seriously @bunnyboy, you need to have faith in yourself.

Especially if you're going this alone without family or a therapist to help you

You can't beat yourself up for something you didn't do

Its not gonna get you anywhere.

NotYourMother: Well it will get you somewhere

It will get you depression and suicidal thoughts

It will invade other aspects of your life and make you miserable

PedoProud: ^ ^ This. What @NotYourMother says.

DontGimmeLolita: For ~~fucks~~ heavens sake someone tell a joke

Oskar: I only know jokes about Michael Jackson.

NotYourMother: Make sure the jokes are funny

No place here for lame jokes

Andrea

In the mirror, she combs her hair, smooths an eyebrow that dares to look as though it might go wild. Her t-shirt, checked for the third time in ten minutes, is still clean and free of holes.

She snorts at the urge to go put on a dress.

"Andrea? You set?" Miguel calls from the bottom of the stairs. His voice doesn't waver, doesn't sound too high or too bright. She doesn't know how he's doing this. Were their roles switched, she's sure she'd either be gushingly positive or violently aggressive—nothing as neutral as "you set?"

The kids are already in the van. She can hear Cara arguing with Miguel as he tries to buckle her into her seat.

"Ca do! Ca do!"

"No, Cara. Sorry. I have to do it."

"CA DOOOOOOO!"

"I need to do it—or Mummy. Do you want Papa or Mummy to do it?"

"MUMMY!"

Andrea slaps him lightly on his rear to move him out of the way.

"You're going to make Papa sad," she tells Cara as she straps her down. "You should be more tolerant of Papa's inability to cater to your every whim."

Cara giggles and kicks at her mother with her miniature pink Uggs.

Andrea looks at Alan. "All set?"

"Yeah." He holds up both fists, each clutching a cootie catcher. "I have three here, too." He tilts his hips and looks down the right side of his booster seat.

"Good man. Wouldn't want to risk a dearth of cootie catchers."

"Yeah. That wouldn't be good." He nods.

She slides the door shut and sits in the passenger seat. After the cool breeze, the sun through the windshield holds the promise of intensity. There's a trace of spring's cold-mud scent coming through the vents.

Miguel's long, thin fingers lightly pat her thigh. She leans back and tries to smile at him. As he draws a breath to say something, Cara bellows over him.

"Dis a book! Dis a book!" She points at the book bag on the floor.

"Yes, love, this is a book. Would you like me to read to you?"

Her little feet kick at the same time as her head nods. It strikes Andrea as an impossible feat, doing the two movements at once, and she has to prevent herself from testing the theory.

"Wild Fings, please," Alan requests.

Twisting uncomfortably so they can both see the pictures, Andrea runs through *Where the Wild Things Are*. It's merely a recitation now: the magic of the story was lost somewhere around the time she memorised the text. She remembers loving the story but can't remember the actual sensation.

The drive to Miguel's sister's is perfectly timed to the two readings of *Where the Wild Things Are* and one rousing rendition of *Free to Be You and Me*. Andrea thinks again about how unfortunate it is that neither Cara nor Alan inherited Miguel's musical abilities, but their enthusiasm is unhindered.

They have not yet realised they can't sing, and she has no intention of telling them.

Lucinda's neighbour is out on her porch, as usual, zipping her wheelchair as close to the driveway as she can.

"Date night again? You two must be in love!"

"Gotta keep it fresh!" Miguel calls back.

They hustle the kids into the house, pretending not to hear the neighbour's inquiries about their evening plans.

While Miguel hoists him over one arm and plucks off his boots, Alan babbles about the cootie catchers to Lucinda. He then heads straight for the living room, his mouth still running on, to share his treasures with his cousins.

Lucinda chuckles. "I'll get his jacket later. He'll get hot eventually." She holds out her arms to take Cara.

Andrea drops the diaper bag just inside the kitchen. "There's some Tylenol in there. She's been a little drooly. I think there might be a tooth coming. And there's a pack of paper for Alan's cootie catchers. He somehow rips them pretty much every time he opens them, and it's the end of the world if he hasn't got an operational one. You remember how to make them?"

"Uh, no." She looks incredulous. "I haven't made one in thirty years!"

Andrea takes Cara into the living room while Miguel gives his sister a refresher course. The kids have built a city of blanket forts, Lego and Playmobile vignettes, and—smack in the middle—a child's inflatable swimming mattress with a stuffed Snoopy napping on it.

"Tia Andrea, would you help me fix this? Alexa played Godzilla on it, but she won't help me fix it."

Andrea settles Cara on her lap while she rebuilds the mashed Lego car and listens to the four older kids all talk at the same time. It doesn't seem to matter to them that the one they're addressing is talking at someone else who also isn't listening. Though the cacophony grinds in Andrea's head, Cara appears to be following each conversation, looking back and forth as though it were a tennis match with several balls. It's mere minutes before she pushes herself off

Andrea's lap and goes to lie on the air mattress with Snoopy.

"Hey, Cara, that's a hospital bed. You're sick!"

Obediently, Cara lies flat on her back, little arms at her side, ready to be examined.

Andrea sneaks back to the kitchen, where Miguel and Lucinda are colouring the inside triangles of a cootie catcher.

"He's not playing with them now," she notes. "They're busy with a patient."

Lucinda picks up a purple crayon. "I'd forgotten about cootie catchers. I used to love these."

"Me, too." Miguel puts his orange crayon back in the box. "Andrea dredged them up last Saturday when I was sleeping in."

She shrugs. "Ended the iPad argument, didn't it? He didn't ask for screen time all day."

"Wish you hadn't called them *cootie catchers*, though. Apparently, the preschool has some issues with the term."

"What should they be called? I didn't realise they had another name."

"The teacher suggested *fortune teller*. I'd never thought about it, either."

Studiously attending to colouring the edge of a triangle, Lucinda casually asks if they're okay.

"We're good." Miguel answers her while locking eyes with Andrea. "There's some stuff we need to talk about, but it's not an emergency. Just thought it would be easier to focus without the kids."

Andrea picks up the stray crayons from the table and tucks them back into their rightful places in their box.

"Okay. Good. It's not that we mind switching date nights. Just wanted to make sure everything was all right."

"All good." He's still looking at Andrea. "Shall we?"

She nods and returns to the living room to kiss the kids goodbye.

Miguel had suggested it would be better to do this away from home, away from the distractions of laundry and dishes and catching up on work.

She thinks maybe he just doesn't want to sully the space they live in.

But he gives her a little smile as they get back into the van and switches the satellite radio to the 80s music he usually barely tolerates.

"Want to eat out, or should we just get something and take it to the hotel room?"

"Whatever you like." She smooths her jeans down over her thighs and straightens the cuffs of her jacket.

"Hmm. Are you actually going to eat?"

Her forehead zings with small flashes of pain. "Erm... I'm not all that hungry."

"'Kay."

They listen to the music. He hums a little, and she casts a glance at him to see if he's making fun, but he doesn't seem to notice that he's humming. After a few blocks, he turns left towards Whole Foods.

"We'll just get snacks."

By the time they've picked up food and checked into the hotel, her head is thudding, and it feels like someone has slapped her hard across her chest and upper arms. She stands back from the front desk, unanchored in the centre of the lobby, guarding the overnight bags and the paper sack of food while Miguel checks in.

He's chosen the nicest hotel in the city, but she can't seem to process the decor or the amenities, as if her eyes are still working but they're not connected to her brain. She recognises, though, that the room is larger than their bedroom. There's a little rush of agoraphobia.

Miguel uses the toilet. She places the bags on the floor and stands, waiting, hands jammed deep in her pockets.

"Do you want to get in the jacuzzi?" he calls as he's washing his hands.

She can't answer him.

He pokes his head around the bathroom doorway. "Andrea?"

"Can we just get this over with?"

He comes to her with his arms out. "Baby, I told you I'm not freaked out about this. Stop worrying so much. I just want to understand it. Your letter didn't give details."

His shoulder is firm and smells like clean laundry. He tightens his arms around her, so she rests her hands on his hips and waits until he lets go.

There are two pieces of paper in his pocket: one is the handwritten letter she left for him two days ago, and the other looks like a list. He lays them on the bed and kicks off his shoes.

"Come here." He pats the bed. "Should I ask questions, or do you want to just talk?"

"Ask the questions."

She doesn't want to sit on the bed, but sitting in the chair would look like she doesn't want to be near him. Then, suddenly, she wants his arms around her again. She wants to rest on his shoulder and have him stroke her hair and whisper to her. She wants him to kiss her cheek.

Sitting on the bed, she straightens the bedclothes beneath her and clamps a pillow over her stomach. There's a large expanse of pinstriped duvet between their bodies.

Leaving the letter where it is, he picks up the other piece of paper but doesn't look at it. "I knew you were worried about something:

your OCD started kicking in a couple of weeks ago. This letter, I guess, explains it?"

Acid burns the back of her throat. She nods.

"Okay. I've been doing a lot of reading in the last two days, but I still need help to understand it all. I think the questions are pretty predictable, but...." He puts the list on her lap so she can read the questions herself.

#1. How long have you known?

Inhaling deeply, she sits taller. Her mind stumbles back through adolescence, almost to childhood. "Since I was about ten, I guess. I didn't admit it to myself until I was more like seventeen."

"What made you admit it to yourself?"

She raises an eyebrow. "What made you admit you were bisexual?"

"Oh." He frowns a little, looking a bit confused. His mouth opens, as if he were going to ask another question, but then he just gestures to the paper.

#2. You say you've never attempted to seduce or assault a child. Why not?

"Because that's rape! I would be a rapist! A child molester! How could I live with myself if I'd done something like that? I'd rather blow my own goddamned fucking brains out!"

For a moment, he's frozen on the other side of the bed. Then he blinks. "That was a bit more... *vehement* than I was expecting. Sorry. Wasn't ready for that." He sighs. "I'm really glad you feel that way, though."

She swipes at the tears on her cheek.

#3. Do you like only kids? How can you have sex with me?

"I don't like only kids. I like adults, too. Adults my age—and kids."

"I read that was possible. So you're non-exclusive."

"Whatever."

"Don't be defensive. I'm not judging you."

"Just didn't know there was a word for it."

"There are lots of words. You'll have to look them all up and tell me which ones we should use."

His face is level with her, his eyes searching. She doesn't know what to think. Her brain has shut down all unnecessary operations.

#4. What made you write the letter now?

Her hands cover her face, and she shuts her eyes to block the rest of the light. She doesn't want to see or hear anything. If she could just sleep for the rest of her life, she would ask for nothing more.

But she has to tell him. If she doesn't, what if...? Her heart thuds at an alarming speed.

"I'm not worried about the kids. I'm not attracted to the kids—"

"That would be the Westermarck effect," he interrupts.

"What's that?"

"A theory explaining why parents aren't usually attracted to their children. Freud said that all children are sexual, like with the Oedipus complex, but Westermarck thought that people who live together don't develop sexual attractions for each other. That's why incest is taboo: it's a psychological oddity."

She has to laugh a little. "You *have* been reading."

"Yup. Sorry. Go on. Why now?"

There's a grey mark on the stucco ceiling. She stares at it for a few seconds. "I'm worried about the kids' friends."

He's quiet for a moment too long, but then she feels his hand on her arm. "We can work around this."

"Yeah? How? Refusing to let them play with their friends in my presence?"

"Well, no. Not like that. Let's not get ridiculous about this. We just have to figure out... I don't know, a way to let the kids have friends but you're still comfortable."

She worries the idea for a bit, thinking about what he said and trying to avoid what he must know. He must know, she thinks. He's not stupid. He can put two and two together. There's no way he can figure it all out, but the elephant in the room will soon start waving its trunk and getting restless.

He rubs her arm. "What about number five?"

#5. Where do we go from here? How can I support you?

"You can't support me, Miguel. You have no idea what this is like. There's no support for this shit. I'm a sick fucking *monster* and you should get the kids away from me!"

In one movement, she flings the pillow away and leaps up. Her fingers rake through her hair as she storms over to the window, looking for space, for anything that isn't right here in front of her. The sun is setting, and the city looks as though it's made of amber. It's too bright. She closes her eyes.

He's behind her. There's a tentative hand on her shoulder.

"I don't know how else to do this," he whispers. "I don't know how to show you that while I don't understand your attraction to kids, this isn't the end of the world. There seems to be a lot of stuff on the internet. It's not just you. This is a thing. I think we can... find you the support you need—whatever you need—and we can find ways of dealing with the kids' friends. I can make sure I'm home, if that's what you want."

She opens her eyes and looks at the city beneath her. "I don't understand why you aren't having a total shit fit about this."

The hand on her shoulder grips harder. "Because I love you. I trust you. I know what it's like to be different about you, to have something about you that society doesn't accept. I can't stop loving you when you haven't done anything wrong. You're still the same person you were before you told me this."

He walks away. She hears him pulling something from his overnight bag.

"I'm going to open the wine. Want some?"

There is a sudden, desperate thirst. "Yeah."

They drink in silence. He returns to the bed, leaning against the padded headboard while she paces.

"You're going through that pretty quick. You should have something to eat." He puts his glass on the bedside table and gets up to empty the grocery bag.

She takes the wedge of camembert on a cracker he holds out.

The wine helps. She refills her glass and slices more cheese.

"Andrea?"

"Yeah?"

"What do you find attractive in a child?"

She stutters through the shock. "No fucking way are we having this discussion."

"Okay. We don't have to."

She takes the wine to the bed and sits down.

He watches her for a moment before coming to sit on the edge of the bed beside her. He removes the wine glass and holds both her hands.

"No, we *do* have to. I need to know, for my sake and everyone else's. I need to know which of the kids' friends it was that set this off."

The humiliation that comes with the tears is physically painful. It curls her into a fetal position, invulnerable around her splintering heart.

When she stops shuddering, his hand rubs her back.

"Lisa," she mutters into her arm.

His hand stops moving. "A girl?"

"Yes."

"So... does that mean you're bisexual, too?"

"I guess so."

"What about boys?"

"Not of any interest."

"What? I can't understand you. Lift your head."

She moves her arm away from her face. "No. Not boys."

"Hmm."

That's all he says for some time. Then he sits up and coaxes her out of her protective ball.

She feels like a boulder has been rolled off her.

"I really want to try the Jacuzzi," he says.

She shakes her head. "I can't be naked. I can't have sex with you right now."

"We don't have to make love."

She shakes her head again.

"Will you sit with me while I'm in there?"

"Sure."

Legs crossed at the knee, she perches on the toilet lid while he lies in the whirling water. The wine has a sweet flavour she hadn't noticed before.

"You know, the thing..." he muses as his hands counter the jet-streams, "the thing that's weirding me out the most is that it's a girl. I don't know why. It did come as a surprise that you like kids—don't get me wrong—but not as much of a shock as it should have." He squints a little at her. "Maybe I kind of knew."

"How did you know?"

"Not sure." His lips purse. "No specific incident comes to mind. No. But the girl thing—that's surprising me more than it should."

"The bisexual is having a hard time with me being bisexual. Miguel, that's just demented."

"Guess I just always thought of you with the male of the species."

She gets up to fetch the bottle.

"Me, too, please." He holds up his glass with a dripping hand. "I was wondering something."

"What's that?"

"Is this why you were iffy about having kids?"

She presses her lips together and nods. The water drops on the floor are too irritating; she wipes them up with toilet paper.

"Would we have had kids if Alan hadn't been a surprise?"

"Probably not. I was a little concerned. Once he was born, though, it didn't seem like an issue."

"And that's why it was okay to have Cara so soon afterwards?"

She tilts her head a little. "Getting old. If we were going to have more than one kid, I couldn't leave it much longer."

"Hmm." His expression turns from thoughtful to serious. "I want you to go on those websites, Andrea. I want you to get support from people who know what they're talking about, what you're going through. Or find a therapist you can trust. I don't think I feel comfortable doing this with just you and me."

Instinct raises alarms, but the thought of Lisa raises sheer panic. "Yeah. I'll try it."

When Miguel has had enough of the Jacuzzi, she goes back to the bed to wait for him. Exhaustion and wine have numbed her, and her eyes start to close. She hears Miguel pulling on some clothes and feels him lie down on the bed beside her, but he doesn't touch her.

"Andrea? Do you love me?"

"Yeah," she responds sleepily, and then realises how it sounds. "Very much."

His voice cracks. "I'm not just a beard?"

Her instinct is to snarl that this is not about him, but she opens her eyes just in time to see him look away. His arms are crossed over his chest.

She dredges up scraps of energy and funnels them together.

"No, you're not just a pedo's beard, Miguel. I love you for who you are, not what you protect me from."

She pulls his head against her breasts and holds him as tightly as she can. His arms clamp around her ribs.

Map Chat: Empathy

DontGimmeLolita: Ugh just got away from one of those asshats on twitter

NotHumbert: Which particular variety of asshat?

bunnyboy: did they want to kill you or did they want you to kill yourself

DontGimmeLolita: Those arent asshats

well they are but I can handle them

This was worse.

a procontact asshat.

Totally blocked him.

PedoProud: Ewww. They disgust me.

DontGimmeLolita: This one was really disgusting

He was all 'we should teach them about sex from birth'

Oskar: Were I inclined to be in favour of the death penalty....

bunnyboy: but doesnt he have a point

NotYourMother: Tread carefully @bunnyboy

NotHumbert: Maybe in some way @bunnyboy but I want you to imagine how that kid would grow up.

They would still not be able to consent and the long-term effects can be terrible.

And how would society treat that child?

Even though its never the child's fault, society treats them as though they're contaminated by the abuse

DontGimmeLolita: Raising kids is about giving them food and shelter and love.

its hard enough giving them everything they need

dont need to give em what they dont need

think about how they feel

Oskar: The person has no point, Bunny Boy. Children have and discover their own sexuality. They do not need the assistance of adults who are only concerned about themselves.

123

NotYourMother: Lets get rid of child porn first

Then we can work on society's views of kid sexuality

PedoProud: I agree with @NotYourMother. We can't even start that conversation until we end the abuse.

DontGimmeLolita: never be able to end all of it

PedoProud: No, but we can try. We can also figure out what minor attractions really are—and *then* we can see what's normal and what's abusive between adults and children.

bunnyboy: i dont know about when i was a baby but i was curious by the time i was like 8

Oskar: You were curious, yes, but you required the knowledge to be fed slowly to you. When an adult forces the knowledge on a child, it is never comfortable for the child. It is like having an entire chocolate cake pushed down your throat. The man who abused me took whatever curiosity I had when I was a child.

bunnyboy: i used to like chocolate cake

Oskar: Yes. It is a good analogy. What is good in itself is not good when it is too much too soon. Suddenly, it is frightening.

NotHumbert: @bunnyboy, we can't take the chance. Maybe the kid would be sexually advanced and be okay with it but there's more of a chance that they wouldn't.

They'd be scared but they'd give in because they felt they had to. Then they're traumatised because they have to keep this huge secret for the adult

DontGimmeLolita: @bunnyboy promise us u'll just block all procontacters right away

Don't talk to them ever

i dont want u learning anything from them

We were all once young like u so we know what u should be like.

bunnyboy: yes mama

DontGimmeLolita: attaboy u know whats good for ya

<u>Xavier</u>

Therapist: Zimmerman, Kelly, MSW, RSW

Name: M^{ac}Donald, Xavier A.

D.O.B: 89/11/15 (age 28)

Therapy: Individual

18/01/10

Client is voluntary. Complaints of anxiety and general depression, with frequent bouts of suicidal thoughts. Symptoms have occurred three times since 15 years ago. Client denies any attempts at suicide.

Not currently taking any prescribed medication. Took Xanax 5 years ago, but stopped due to side effects. Currently occasional (weekly) recreational use of alcohol and marijuana. No major or long-term health problems. Sleep erratic during "intense periods" of depression and or anxiety.

Client is not aware of any mental illness in his family.

Client was punctual, neatly dressed and groomed. He exhibited nervous habits, namely bitten nails and scratching at the inside of his right arm. He answered questions succinctly but with long pauses before his response.

Client wishes to control the social anxiety and depression to allow for more self-confidence and furthering job prospects. Client often feels "judged" when in public, without justification, since two weeks ago.

Client is in a long-term (3-year) co-habitating relationship with male partner (Jack) who is one and a half years older than the client. Long-term (4 years) employment in bank. Financially stable.

Weekly Goal: Client will make a list of situations in which he feels uncomfortable.

18/01/17

Client punctual and well-groomed.

Homework was neatly hand-written in a small notebook. Client tore the pages out of the notebook but then decided to read aloud himself. During the week, he noticed discomfort in places like the grocery store and the lunch room at work. Also, a great deal of discomfort with his partner, as well as with an acquaintance.

Client chose to focus on the partner this week.

Client stated he often does things he is not interested in doing because "it's easier than dealing with Jack all pissed off. I can handle it when I'm not getting what I want, but not when he's all sulky." Situations included eating at restaurants where the food did not appeal to the client and going to a nightclub where the clientele were "a little skanky" and "didn't respect personal boundaries".

When asked how this affected his own emotions, the client noted that he frequently held grudges against his partner. Client admitted to a "mental tally" of the occasions when he had given into his partner's desires. Client does not know how he plans to use this tally in the future.

At the termination of the session, the client noted in passing that another situation where he gave in to his partner was in bed. Due to time constraints, this matter will be discussed at the next session.

Weekly Goal: Use the self-soothing phrase "I am comfortable" in situations where the client has assessed there is no reason to be uncomfortable.

2018/01/24

Client punctual and neat.

Situational discomfort still affecting client, inhibiting social contact. Discussed the likelihood of strangers knowing enough about him to judge. Client belongs to a racial minority (Caucasian/Asian) but did not feel he was being judged for that, as he says he knows what that looks and feels like. Client could not explain what he felt was being judged.

Client stated that the self-soothing phrase had been effective in impersonal interactions such as at the grocery store and movie theatre. When he felt people were judging him, he repeated the phrase "like a mantra and felt better". Assessment of the situation led him to believe he was "just being paranoid, or projecting or something".

When asked what he could have been projecting, the client noted that he often judges people for their social behaviour. Examples given: "rudeness", "public displays of affection". Clothing, social status, etc. are not judged.

The phrase was not successful in situations involving his partner or partner's social group, or at work.

Client stated that he rarely wanted to have sex with his partner, that "once every couple of weeks" would be his preference, rather than every day. His interest in the partner is "more emotional". The client likes to be affectionate and social with his partner, but "gives in" to the partner's request for sex because the partner gets "whiny".

Client stated that his main complaint is the partner's insistence that both of them orgasm. Client would be content with just making his partner orgasm. "Sometimes, I just don't feel like cumming with him. Just not in that mood."

Strategies for compromise were discussed.

I believe the client is holding something back on something he would like to discuss. I will wait until the client is more familiar and comfortable with me before pursuing the matter.

Weekly Goal: Make specific note of situations with partner. Where possible, avoid "giving in" without first making an effort towards compromise.

2018/01/31

Client well-groomed and punctual.

Client seemed nervous at the beginning of the session, fidgeting with clothes and shifting position. When asked if there was anything he wanted to talk about, the client inquired about the legal guidelines for mandatory reporting. When told the official rules and this therapist's personal guidelines, the client asked several times for assurance and clarification about "no crime committed" and "no threat to himself or others".

Client stated that he is sexually attracted to boys aged 12-15. He repeated, several times, that he has not touched a child sexually, does not view child pornography and believes adult/child sex to be abusive in all situations.

Client stated that he felt hiding his attraction would hinder therapy.

Client denied that his relationship problems may be connected to his minor attraction.

Client declined to add situations with children to his list of socially-uncomfortable situations.

Due to time constraints, the previous week's topic of discomfort with partner was not discussed.

I was shocked by the client's announcement and am concerned my shock was evident. If memory serves, there is recent research in this area. I will seek professional support re: hebephilia.

Weekly Goal: Continue self-soothing and communicating with partner.

2018/02/07

N.B. Professional support obtained from Centre for Addiction and Mental Health, Toronto, ON.

Client was punctual and nicely dressed. He appeared to have put more effort into grooming than usual.

Client appeared quite nervous and tired.

Client asked if this therapist had any questions regarding his "pedophilia". Information from CAMH was shared with the client; the terms *hebephilia* and *ephebophilia* were used thereafter.

As background, the client stated that he had begun "normal kid sex exploration" with other children at age 12. Homosexuality discovered around that age. Hebephilia and ephebophilia discovered around age 17-19 when he realised he was no longer attracted to the individuals he had once found attractive.

Current teleiophilia AOA 24-35 (male only).

Client confirmed he had not been sexually abused during childhood or adolescence.

Client related a story about his first boyfriend. Sexual attraction diminished as the boy physically matured.

Adult pornography not used for masturbation as the client is worried he may think it would be better porn if a child was involved.

Concern is hypothetical as client has not tested himself.

Transcript Excerpt
M^(ac)Donald, Xavier A.

K.Z: You had said, in our last session, that your minor attraction might be somehow connected to your relationship problems with Jack. What made you say that?

X.M: Your reaction when I said I was a pedo. You seemed surprised, and now you seem to be more interested in it than anything else. I assume you think it's the cause of everything.

K.Z: My interest is guided by your reaction.

X.M: So we're feeding off each other?

K.Z: That's a normal human interaction, so, yes, I'd have to agree with you.

X.M: (*pause*) I told you about it because I didn't want to hold anything back from you. I've totally had it with feeling nervous and uncertain and... shaky all the time. I just need your help to fix this. I want to get on with living. I don't want to be skulking in corners for the rest of my life.

K.Z: Have you told Jack about your other attractions?

X.M: Only the adult ones. We have an open relationship.

K.Z: Who else have you told about your minor attractions?

X.M: No one. Ever. Only you.

K.Z: Why haven't you told Jack?

X.M: It's not the kind of thing you tell people.

K.Z: How do you think he'd react?

X.M: Beat the shit out of me.

K.Z: Is Jack often violent?

X.M: Never. But I'm a pedo, and that's how the world deals with pedos.

K.Z: Not *pedophile...*

X.M: Right. Yeah, right. *Hebephile* and *ephebophile.*

K.Z: How would you like Jack to respond? If you told him, what would you like him to do or say?

X.M: Beating me up is fine.

K.Z: Do you enjoy being beaten? Are you a masochist?

X.M: No, of course not. I hate pain. Never even got into fights as a kid 'cause I can't take it. But that's what I deserve.

K.Z: Why do you deserve that?

X.M: For being attracted to kids.

K.Z: Have you ever sexually assaulted a minor?

X.M: I told you, no! I've never touched a kid—not since I was one, anyway. No, but if I told Jack, he'd know that I sometimes think about them when I'm with him. Sorta...

K.Z: What do you mean by that?

X.M: By what?

K.Z: Do you always think about minors when you're having sex with an adult?

X.M: Only with Jack, and only sometimes.

K.Z: What would make you think about a minor when you're with Jack?

X.M: When he wants to have sex and I don't. Sometimes, it's the only way I can cum.

K.Z: Is the orgasm pleasurable in those circumstances?

X.M: No. He just won't lay off until I cum, though, so it makes my life easier (*sighs*) to think about a kid.

K.Z: Do you fantasise about a certain kid?

X.M: No. Just parts of some... a made-up kid.

K.Z: Does the sex, in these specific situations, bring any pleasure for you?

X.M: No way. I'm usually so pissed off that I just want to get out of that bed.

K.Z: What are you pissed off about?

X.M: Having to fuck when I'm not in the mood. Being forced to think about kids just so I don't have to put up with Jack's bullshit insecurity afterwards.

K.Z: Are there ever times when you do want to have sex with Jack?

X.M: Yeah, sometimes.

K.Z: Would you consider those times to be pleasurable sex?

X.M: Yeah, it's good, then. We cuddle afterwards. Pillow talk, you know.

K.Z: If you're in the mood to have sex, do you have to think about children to orgasm?

X.M: No, I don't think about them then. I just think about Jack—what he's doing to me, what I'm doing to him.

K.Z: You said the fantasies involve a (*flips paper*) "made-up kid". Is there a real child you're attracted to?

X.M: (*long pause*) There are two that I'm attracted to, one that I think I might be in love with. But that's mostly fantasy 'cause I don't see either of them anymore.

K.Z: Why don't you see them anymore?

X.M: I stay the fuck away from anyone like that. They don't need to deal with the likes of me. They don't need to see me looking at them with fucking puppy-dog eyes. Shit. They don't deserve that.

K.Z: You're suddenly quite angry.

X.M: Fuck. Yeah. Yeah, I'm pissed.

K.Z: About what? What just happened that made you angry?

X.M: (*pause*) It's just a guy I know.

K.Z: A minor?

X.M: An adult. The co-worker I told you about before.

K.Z: What about him makes you angry?

X.M: (*pause*) Nothing. It's not important.

End of transcript excerpt

Weekly goal: Continue self-soothing. Communication discomfort to partner.

2018/02/14

Client punctual but not as neatly groomed as previously. Unshaven (1-2 days) and circles under eyes.

Client says sleep is "normal" (6-7 hours per night, no disturbances).

Self-soothing in most public situations still successful.

Client was unable to communicate discomfort to his partner, as "it would be too much effort to deal with the inevitable fallout". Client complained that the partner was demanding of sexual and affectionate physical contact. Client stated that the partner, if denied, will either "smother me with 'kindness' and 'understanding' [client used air quotes for both words] until I give in" or partner will "sulk".

Client reconfirmed he was physically and romantically attracted to the partner, but they have "different levels of needs".

Client stated that he masturbates daily, though his sexual needs involving a partner are infrequent ("almost never", though previously the client stated he enjoyed physical relations with his partner approximately twice a month).

Client denied feeling uncomfortable about any aspects of his homosexuality.

Client stated his partner had made Valentine's Day plans for the evening. As client was not privy to the details, he stated he had no problem with partner's plans and didn't want to give input. Client didn't see it as an opportunity to assert his preferences.

Though I am more comfortable with the client's sexual orientation, I am still feeling a little frustrated. I am convinced there is still something being avoided.

Weekly Goal: Attempt to communicate discomfort to partner again.

2018/02/21

Client punctual but ill-groomed again, exhibiting signs of nervousness and possible sleep-deprivation.

Client immediately said he was ready to discuss the co-worker brought up in the previous session.

Client related a reportable offence that was committed by said co-worker.

Client was very upset that he had waited to report this offence. Client stated he hoped the victim would never forgive him.

Client ended the session ten minutes early because he wanted to report the abuse before he had time to change his mind.

Self-soothing and social anxiety were not discussed during this session.

Formal report made to local police. Report #17-CS946833

Transcript Excerpt
M^{ac}Donald, Xavier A.

K.Z: You said you were ready to discuss your co-worker, the one who makes you angry.

X.M: Yeah.

K.Z: What made you decide to discuss him with me?

X.M: I think I need to report him. I know, I know, I'm a goddamned hypocrite, but I think I'm gonna do it anyway.

K.Z: What makes you a hypocrite?

X.M: Actually, not quite the same, but at least I'm not screwing a kid.

K.Z: Is he having sex with a minor?

X.M: Yeah. Yeah. He told me this whole long story about how it's not against her will because he never forces her to do anything. He made it sound like he was some chivalrous knight in fucking shining armour who mentored her by helping her learn about her sexuality. Told me how it was okay because any time she didn't want to do anything, he'd just back off and try again later. He made sure she orgasmed each time—so he's not a bad guy.

K.Z: You disagree with him that it makes everything okay?

X.M: Yes! I know for a fucking *fact* that it doesn't make everything okay! Just because someone isn't screaming "Rape!" doesn't make it okay. (*pause*) Maybe it means she was just too tired to fight him off anymore.

K.Z: Do you ever feel like a rape victim after you've been with Jack?

X.M: (*pause*) That's different. We're two adults. I agree to have sex with him. She's too young to understand what it all means, what her body is really doing to her mind.

K.Z: Because a minor is endangered, I'm obligated to report this.

X.M: Be my guest. I'm going to report it, too. Right after this session. It makes me sick to think about what he's doing to her.

K.Z: What's his name?

X.M: Here, give me the pen. I'll write everything down for you. Here's his address and the school he works at. I don't know her name, but she's fair-haired and a little chubby. Grade 10.

K.Z: Thank you. This is being entered into the official record, and I will report to the police immediately after this session.

X.M: Good.

K.Z: How are you feeling right now?

X.M: Good. Good. (*pause*) I've known for about two months now....

K.Z: Why did he tell you about it? Does he know about your minor attraction?

X.M: No, he was just bragging. I think he's told a couple of other guys about it, too. He's really... (*sighs*) really proud of himself.

K.Z: Xavier, that seems to upset you. You're all balled up in your chair. What's making you cry?

X.M: I've been thinking about it the whole time. I've let her be abused for like two months longer than necessary. (*pause*) I feel like I've been the one abusing her.

K.Z: Why do you feel like that? (*pause*) A shrug is an evasive response. Try to pinpoint it.

X.M: Can't.

K.Z: Why not?

X.M: Because I let her feel like this for so long when she didn't have to!

K.Z: How do you think she feels?

X.M: (*pause*) *He* says she's in love with him.

K.Z: What are your thoughts on that?

X.M: She might be, but it's more likely... what's it? Stockholm Syndrome? When you're in love with your abuser?

K.Z: Yes, Stockholm Syndrome. What makes you think that?

X.M: She can't be in love with him. Not for real. When you're fourteen, you don't know what love really is. When I was fourteen, I thought I was really mature and knew everything then, but in reality the relationships were about, I guess, well, me. I was interested in getting what my own body wanted and needed—what my heart wanted and needed, too. It was all about sex and having someone show they liked me. I needed the love and affection, but I had to figure out who I wanted to receive it from.

And, besides, it doesn't matter that she's in love with him. If people find out, they're going to treat her differently, like it was her fault. She'll feel dirty for the rest of her life.

145

Even if she moves someplace where no one knows her, it'll be in her head forever.

I liked Andy before, but now he seems like a real asshole. He said he told her she was in love with him, and he was right. It's like some manipulative... patriarchal, arranged-marriage bullshit. *I'll tell you to love me and you will, and I'll tell you **how** to love me.*

K.Z: You used a mocking tone for that last sentence. Why?

X.M: Shouldn't have, I guess. It's absolutely serious. Nothing to make fun of.

End of transcript excerpt

2018/02/28

Client arrived three minutes late and wearing work-out clothing. When asked if he'd been to the gym, the client said he had slept late and didn't have time to dress for the day.

Client stated he had called in sick for work for the previous two days but denied being ill. He stated his need for "mental health days". He claimed he is taking "a staycation".

Client brought up a news article about his co-worker's arrest. He stated he was pleased the perpetrator had been caught. Client's physical demeanour and facial expressions contradicted this statement. During the session, the client bit his fingernails to the point of bleeding.

Self-soothing phrase was not applicable this week as he had not left his house except to go to work. He claims to have avoided his co-workers all week.

Client's general mood is much lower than previously.

Client did not "feel like chatting today". Asked for relaxation exercises and tips on meditation.

Despite the client's downswing in mood, I feel as though we may have finally cracked the shell of the core issue.

2018/03/07

Client is still functional but displaying signs of depression: lack of grooming, tearful outbursts, lethargy. Stated his mood is similar at home and at work. Against medical advice, client refused a referral to receive a prescription for medication.

When asked about the depression, the client looked down at himself and said he wasn't "worth any effort".

Client expressed a desire to leave the session early but was convinced to stay. The remaining time was used for relaxation exercises. Though the client was calmer by the end of the session, professional intervention may be required. As yet, he does not appear to be a threat to himself or anyone else.

Weekly goal: The client has been asked to make a personal timeline of the past 10 years, adding any

Transcript Excerpt

M^{ac}Donald, Xavier A.

K.Z: Why aren't you worth the effort?

X.M: (*pause*) It'll fuck up again, even if I fix it.

K.Z: What will fuck up again?

X.M: Everything.

K.Z: Can you unpack that a little?

X.M: (*pause*) I'm a pedo who let a girl get assaulted. I'm a pedo who will probably do that same shit to some other kid, someday, telling myself it's okay because they came as often as I did so it's all equal. I'm such a chickenshit that I keep a job I don't really like because my fucking boyfriend thinks "it works well with our life-style" and I don't even have the goddamned sex life that I want—even though it's legal for me to be a queer now. It doesn't matter what I do. Everyone tells me how to live my life. I'm a shitty human being with no spine and why bother putting in effort for someone like that? Let the people in the fucking shopping mall judge me, for Christ's sake! They're right! Whatever they're thinking, they're right! My parents were right! I'm a moral fuck-up!

End of transcript excerpt

2018/03/14

Client did not show up for regular appointment.

Client is not returning phone messages.

2018/03/16

Therapy of Xavier A. M^acDonald terminated due to client's successful suicide.

Client apparently mailed the attached timeline just before his death.

March 13, 2018

Dear Kelly,

Thank you for being my therapist. You're quite a good one.

Sorry for missing the last session. A money order for the fee is enclosed.

Here's the homework you asked me to do.

2007: *Nothing much happened here. I was 18 years old and had recently discovered I was a monster.*

2007-2017: *I convinced myself I wasn't a monster.*

January 1, 2017: *I learned there were other monsters in the world. I did nothing about it.*

March 15, 2017: *I am still a monster.*

Sincerely, Xavier M^acDonald

MAP Chat: Religion

NotHumbert: My mother is driving me nuts.

> She's trying to get me to go to church with her

PedoProud: Not a proponent of religion?

NotHumbert: Um, no.

> And it's not a proponent of me either.

PedoProud: I don't think many MAPs are religious. Are we? Does anyone go to church?

Oskar: I do.

NotYourMother: I'm very active in my church

bunnyboy: temple

DontGimmeLolita: i coulda guessed that @NotYourMother and @Oskar were religious

> Wouldn't have said that about u @bunnyboy

NotYourMother: @bunnyboy What do you get from attending temple?

bunnyboy: my life

> my moms scarier than g-d

PedoProud: Oh, I was about to commiserate with you about temple, but you mean Jewish synagogue. I was thinking about all the times I was dragged to a Hindu temple by relatives. I wasn't raised in a particularly religious family though.

DontGimmeLolita: Hindu temple has always sounded interesting

if I had to go to a temple that is.

Oskar: I enjoy church. I am able to communicate with God and participate in my community at the same time. In my country, religion is part of society. It would be uncomfortable to go without it.

NotHumbert: But don't you have problems with people that hate you for your sexuality?

Oskar: Sexuality does not come up as a topic of conversation. It is church. There is worship. There is no sex.

bunnyboy: that immaculate conception business wasnt real

NotHumbert: Yeah I know @Oskar but I mean, you know they'd hate you if they knew.

NotYourMother: I don't agree with everything my church teaches

I teach my children differently at home

The big thing I teach my children is that the love at church is more important than the hate.

PedoProud: That sounds lovely, @NotYourMother. It's a beautiful approach.

DontGimmeLolita: that's what the priest said.

NotYourMother: Even priests are fallible

I also teach my children that fallibility shouldn't be hidden or excused

bunnyboy: @NotHumbert you said the people would hate @Oskar if they knew

if i worried about everyone hating me id die

g-d made me

this is who i have to be even if they hate me

NotYourMother: Out of the mouths of babes.

DontGimmeLolita: so @NotHumbert Will you go to church with your mom?

NotHumbert: Probably

Like @bunnyboy said, it's the safe alternative

Hugh

Hugh wakes with the sun, slowly, pleasantly rising from sleep. He stretches a little, to remind his body it needs to follow the example of his brain. Awake, he sits on the edge of the bed and slides his feet into sheepskin slippers.

"Good morning, God. Thank you for another day," he whispers. "I appreciate the gift."

He waits for a few seconds but, as was, is and (he suspects) ever shall be, there's no response. From his bedside table, he takes a small wine-coloured book, which lists the lessons of the day, and then finds Lamentations in the black leather-bound King James Bible--a long-ago gift from his Confirmation.

How doth the city sit solitary, that was full of people! how is she become as a widow! she that was great among the nations, and princess among the provinces, how is she become tributary!
She weepeth sore in the night, and her tears are on her cheeks: among all her lovers she hath none to comfort her:

all her friends have dealt
treacherously with her, they are
become her enemies.

"Well. They certainly know how to
start the day on a cheery note."

He finishes reading the lesson before
standing up and stretching once more.

That's quite the outfit, sweetie.

Hugh touches his lilac ascot and then
the lilac-and-gold urn on the living room
mantelpiece. "I chose it because it matches
you."

When did you get it?

"Yesterday. I hid it in the bottom of
the bag. Knew you'd be snide about it."

Hmph.

Hugh strides out of the living room,
denying David the opportunity to continue the
commentary.

Hugh likes this new aspect of their
relationship. Had he been brave enough to
walk out of the room during the previous fifty-
two years, his life would have been much
easier.

In the kitchen, he assembles a plate of whole-grain toast and grapefruit, pours a mug of coffee and a glass of milk, and places everything on an inlaid teak tray. Resting his hands on the edge of the counter, Hugh closes his eyes and whispers, "For that which I am about to receive, may the Lord make me truly thankful. Amen."

He carries the tray to the living room.

Turn on the breakfast news, please.

"It's Sunday."

Oh. Got a tad befuddled there.

Hugh flips open the "morning" lid of his pill box and dumps the seven pills onto his breakfast tray.

If it's Sunday, why is the iron pill there? You don't take iron on lazy days.

In response, Hugh crunches a bite of toast.

Hugh Jones-Smith.

"It's Thursday."

Why the deception? Messing with the dead is generally frowned upon.

"It's a good day. I don't want to ruin it with news of the world crashing and burning."

What if you miss something good?

"I'll take my chances."

What shall we talk about, then?

"Silence is an option."

One that never appealed to me. Tell me what you're doing today.

"No."

Whyever not?

"Because I'm going to church and I don't want to listen to your bullshit about it."

To church! What possessed you to decide to do that?

"You died. Now I can go to church."

There is stony silence.

To make amends, Hugh gets up and puts a CD on the stereo: Beethoven's *Ninth*. As the familiar notes swell into the room, Hugh steels his ears against the noise. He still hates Beethoven.

Bribery will get you nowhere, dear heart.

David's voice is sulky, though softer. For all his cock-of-the-walk blustering, Hugh thinks, the boy always was a pushover.

He picks up the silver teaspoon and digs out a pink grapefruit section.

Yellow grapefruit is healthier.

"But not as sweet."

You'll get diabetes and die.

"If I don't have diabetes yet, I doubt a grapefruit will be the tipping point."

You never know.

"Well, then, you'll just have to make room for me on the mantelpiece."

You should buy your urn now. Make sure it doesn't clash with me. Why are you wolfing your food? Rushing to cleanse your sins?

"I'm not going to church until this evening. Need to do a lot of errands this morning."

Ooooh! Are we having a party?

"Easter dinner. Andrew, Michel, Bianca and Louis, Mary."

What about Cecil?

Hugh raises his eyes to the mantelpiece. "He's no longer with us, darling. Did you forget? He passed away three weeks ago."

Oh. Yes. I forgot. You wore that charcoal suit.

"Oh, give it a rest."

I'm just saying, you look so much better in blue.

Hugh shuts the Volvo door and turns the key. He takes out the Sandy Denny CD and slides in Steeleye Span. He feels like singing today.

Though it's not a day for singing. It's supposed to be a sombre day—at least, this evening will be sombre. During daylight hours, humans are allowed to pretend they don't understand what's coming.

The grocery store is ridiculously crowded. He puts on his headphones and turns on his MP3 player: the music will be a soothing safeguard against stupid people, with the added benefit of being able to blame the music when he doesn't hear them.

A large ham—just the packaged kind, not the kind with a bone—and a small tofurkey, because Mary is vegetarian. Rice, because Andrew still believes it's healthier than potatoes, and potatoes, because Michel is a traditionalist; a tin of stuffed grapevine leaves as a nod to the adventurous eaters in the group. Apart from that, they'll have to suffer: David was the one with the interest in cooking. Hugh's big effort will be to make a pavlova for dessert. He can make the base on Saturday, so he's not too tired when everyone arrives on Sunday.

He picks his way through the store, avoiding any crowded aisle. Most of the shoppers ignore him, moving around him as if he weren't there. A couple of them, both with white hair, nod at him; a gaggle of teenage girls glance at his lilac ascot and giggle behind their hands.

You laugh at me, he thinks, but you should have seen David's wardrobe. Now *that* was gay.

Do they still flop their wrists behind gay men's backs? He doesn't want to turn around to look, though as the last one passes, his eye catches a ringlet of soft blonde hair and a narrow waist over thin hips, a flash of flesh just above the waistband of her jeans. Breath sticks in his chest.

He pretends to study a neon-green tin on the shelf in front of him, waiting until he's sure they've turned the corner.

In the freezer section, he picks up a package of frozen bread dough that he can just pop in the oven to make hot dinner rolls, and then goes to the bakery to get a croissant for his lunch.

The sky is clear and blue as he loads the grocery bags into the trunk. Hugh turns his face towards the sun, grateful for the tepid warmth.

On a whim, he turns right at the main intersection and heads out of town to the nursery, where he spends a quarter-hour wandering through the greenhouse before purchasing two pots of tulips, two of hyacinths and four of daffodils. For the first time in over a year, the living will outnumber the dead in his apartment.

At home, he puts the groceries away before making two trips to bring in the flowers.

Oh my, did someone die?

"Shit. Lilies. I should have bought some lilies, too."

The coffee table is full; he reshelves some books, tosses the old New Yorker magazines into the recycling bin and puts the glass statue on top of the fridge.

All the plants go on the coffee table, except for one pot of daffodils for the front windowsill.

"There." He admires the colours and inhales deeply.

A fine garden, old boy.

"It's life-affirming, isn't it?"

I wouldn't know.

He puts on a podcast while he eats his chicken and tomato croissant. David prattles, heedless of the other sounds in the room.

I suppose you put Miracle Whip on it, too?

"You suppose correctly."

What an unhealthy lunch.

"Got a cupcake for dessert, too," Hugh lies, hoping to incense David into silence.

You never! Whatever happened to living a healthy lifestyle?

Hugh glares at the urn. "More focussed on actually living, right now." He washes down two pills with water.

Oh, sure. Blame me for dying.

"I'm sure you would have evolved, too, if you'd been given the time. You'd have given in to dietary and physical insouciance, just like me."

Never. Just look at the science. Controlling one's diet is the best way to guarantee a long life.

"Is this the same science that misdiagnosed your lymphoma?"

A fluke. You shouldn't be eating all that shit. You'll get fat and die of a heart attack.

"Are you going to let me listen to this podcast or what?"

Fine.

David sighs from his urn. Hugh takes another bite, the buttery pastry flaking on his tongue for a split second before the creamy tang of the Miracle Whip hits.

What did you get for dinner?

"Nothing. I'm going out."

What? Where?

"Just out."

To the Old Mill?

"Nothing like that."

Where to?

"Just… to... someone's house."

Cecil's? Wait, no, I remember. Andrew's?

"Nope. No one you know."

You've made new friends?

"What did you expect?"

Hmph. Will the food be good?

"Probably not. I'm expecting… *filling* rather than *good*. It's more about the company."

I'd hold out for better food.

He takes the last bite of his sandwich and stands up, still chewing.

You're seriously going to get that cupcake?

"Gonna eat it in the kitchen so you can't hound me."

I'll yell.

"If I couldn't hear you from there when you were alive, I certainly won't be able to just 'cause you're dead," he taunts as he walks out.

In the kitchen, he perches on the edge of a chair. "Dear God, thank you for the morning, for this body, which allows me to leave the house, for the continued independence."

His mind flips back through the morning's activities.

"Thank you for creating beautiful flowers in spring, to remind us of life—and thank you for creating humans who can make butter and Miracle Whip that taste so good together. Please bless David's soul. Amen."

He stands, pushes the chair back in and puts his lunch dishes in the dishwasher.

Did you eat it?

"And loved it."

What are you doing now?

"Emails. And I think there's a text that I didn't check. I thought I heard it ding while I was making lunch."

Don't work in the study. Bring the laptop in here.

"Of course. I want to enjoy these flowers."

And me.

"And you, my love."

By 1:30, Hugh starts to feel the heaviness at the back of his neck, the fogginess of his brain when he tries to think.

"Naptime."

Sweet dreams of me, honey. Think about how I looked naked on silk sheets.

Before he lies down, Hugh removes the lilac ascot and drapes it over the back of a wooden chair. In the mirror, he admires the glint of the silver cross around his neck.

At 4:00, Hugh closes his book and goes to take a shower. He blow-dries his thin white hair, puts on his charcoal-grey suit and a white shirt. Briefly, his hand rests on the tie rack, but then he goes to the tallboy dresser and chooses a plum-coloured ascot.

Mm-mmm.

"Thank you."

Must be quite the friends to deserve the likes of you at their table—and all in exchange for "filling food".

"Quite nice, yes."

You're hiding something, darling.

"No, just exploring something that didn't interest you."

David gasps. *A woman?*

"No."

A... girl?

168

"For fuck's sake, David! Of course not!"

Alright, alright... I know you said, but I was just checking.

"You know me better than that."

I thought I did but, for the life of me, I can't figure out what you're doing.

"I'm going to church. It's Maundy Thursday, which is kind of the beginning of Easter. I'm eating a Passover supper at the church, attending the service and then staying for the Garden Watch."

What's a Garden Watch when it's at home?

"We wait until midnight. Christ asked if anyone would stay awake with him. The goal is to do better than the Disciples."

David is silent.

"No comments from the peanut gallery?"

Call me gobsmacked.

Not for long, I bet, Hugh thinks to himself.

So, you're going to sit up for a dead guy who wouldn't have accepted you, with people who don't accept you, and eat shit for dinner. Is this what you're telling me?

"Not all of them object to gays, David."

But they wouldn't let you be married, even though it was so ridiculously important to you.

"Darling, we've seen so much change since Stonewall. Be pleased with that. This is about me and God, not the people in the pews."

Or the pedo in a dress in front of the altar?

"Being a priest does not mean one is a pedo."

Hmph.

"Must go. I've checked the back door and turned off the lights."

Hugh, honey...

"Yes?"

I'm just worried about you.

"Nothing's killed me yet, love."

Hugh kisses his fingertips and touches them to the gold filigree on the urn.

"Shall be back around 12:30."

Be safe.

In the church basement that smells of dust and old coffee, Hugh holds out his $5 donation to the woman at the table by the door.

"Hello!" With one hand, she takes the bill but holds it in mid-air, and with the other hand she points to her name tag. "My name is Wendy. Have I seen you here before?"

"Just started coming a couple of Sundays ago."

"Welcome, then! So glad you could join us. Here's a name tag, so everyone can get to know you—and there's no charge for newcomers." She hands the bill back with the name tag sticker and a Sharpie.

"Thank you very much."

By the time he has written his name and stuck the label on his lapel, there's a silver-haired man named John, a few years younger than Hugh, standing beside him. The man clasps his hand warmly and leads him to a table of other senior citizens. In the confusion of more greetings and yelling over the scuffling of chairs, a young man in a wrinkled white shirt and torn black jeans plops a plate on the table in front of Hugh. On the plate, placed at quarter-hours, is a breaded cutlet, a round scoop of mashed potatoes, a small pile of French-cut green beans and a slice of white bread with a paper-wrapped butter pat resting on top of it. Another teenager, similarly dressed but reeking of body spray, slops ice water into Hugh's glass.

Hugh grins. Nothing has changed in sixty-five years.

Suddenly, everything is silent. The people at Hugh's table all turn to the broad-faced woman at the front of the hall. She wears a loose black suit, with a white collar at her throat. Her hands are clasped in front of her.

"Let us pray," she commands. "Bless us, O Lord, and these, Your gifts, which we are about to receive, from Your bounty, through Christ Our Lord. Amen."

They all murmur "Amen", and some of them cross themselves, and then there's the clatter of silverware and the clamour of voices again.

Hugh spends the meal listening to John, the man who led him to the table, talk about the church garden. Things are pushing up already, apparently: crocii in the last of the snow piles. He hopes the scilla in the lawns will do just as well as last year, and the new rosebushes in the WWI graveyard look like they've survived the winter.

Hugh cuts the food into small bites. As he predicted, it's filling and marginally-satisfying, though nothing to write home about. He'll tell David about it tomorrow: it will give him something to gripe about.

While the adults eat apple pie with vanilla ice cream and sip tepid, weak tea, the youngest children stand on the stage and sing "Brother, Sister, Let Me Serve You". Their high voices are unintelligible but sweet to Hugh's ear.

Upstairs in the nave, John invites Hugh to sit in "his" pew, along with his wife and adult daughter.

The last of the evening light is at the very bottom of the stained-glass windows. Hugh tries to settle on the hard wood.

"They need cushions for people like us," John's wife says, her hand resting on Hugh's arm. "We've been saying that for years, but it just never seems to happen. Our old bones do penance at every service."

Hugh lightly pats her hand. "I'm sure I've committed enough sins that an hour of penance won't go amiss."

She chuckles softly and turns to face the altar again.

Hugh fumbles his way through the opening prayers, the language odd in his mouth after so many years.

Each congregant is given a taper to hold, lighting it from their neighbour's, passing the flame along the pews. The stained-glass windows are entirely dark now, the Biblical figures eerily trapped within the black lead lines. Hugh focuses on his flame during the Gospel reading and then, as instructed, he gustily blows it out.

The blackness and dead silence in the church takes his breath away. From somewhere in the balcony, a single voice intones a hymn in a minor key.

Slowly, carefully, holding onto each other and the pew ends for support, the congregation makes its way out of the nave and into the bright narthex.

Hugh blinks. John's hand clamps down on his shoulder, surprising him. "You'll be staying for the Garden Watch? At least for an hour or so?"

Hugh hesitates, opening himself to the energy around him. *Jesus? I'd like to stay. Is it all right if I stay?*

There's no confirmation—but no refusal.

"I think I'm good for the whole Watch," he tells John.

"For now, you can go wherever feels right—anywhere in the church," John says. "We all meet up at 11:45 in the garden. You have a coat? Good. It's mighty cold out there at midnight."

The congregants who are staying split off into groups: to the basement for more food and conversation, outside in the church yard to see the sky, and back into the black nave for private prayer and reflection.

Hugh smiles as John introduces him to a few people, and then he excuses himself to return to the darkness of the church.

He slides into the first pew he can make out in the dark and, ignoring his body's complaints, sinks onto the kneeler. His hands automatically clasp, but he changes his mind; folding his arms onto the hymnal rest, he buries his face in his charcoal-grey sleeves. He can see nothing, even if he opens his eyes, and his hearing is dulled by the shoulders of his jacket. Hunched over like this, he can feel the tightness along his stretched spine, the pressure of his knees on the Naugahyde padding of the kneeler.

Jesus, here I am again. I have no idea whether you want me here or not: you're silent on the matter. In any case, this doesn't feel wrong. I'm going to continue until something changes. Let me know if you'd like something different. Like for me to go to hell. You've said nothing about sexuality. There's some stuff in the Old Testament, but you said you were giving us new rules. There were no new rules about me loving David. Humans have old rules about it, which is why I left the church in the first place, but you've never said anything about it one way or the other.

And that other thing... yeah, that one. I don't need a sign from you to know that acting on that would break the "love one another as I have loved you" rule.

I remember that time I felt you were angry with me, when I stopped talking to my mother. I remember it felt good when I finally decided to listen to her rant and rail, and then we started talking again. It took a long time, and it was very difficult not to be furious with her, but then things got better. She and David ended up getting along relatively well, all things considered. See, after that, I felt like you weren't angry anymore.

You haven't left me in seventy-nine years, even when I was making no outward commitment to you. While I couldn't feel your love like I did when I was a child, I didn't feel abandoned.

We're told to ask for signs. I've asked many times for signs, and you don't give them to me, so I'm just going to take this relationship on faith.

You made me. You made me male and good at business and not good at cooking. You made me short and slight and gave me skinny thighs. You made me gay and a good husband—according to David, anyway. You made me attracted to young girls, but you made me moral, as well.

If you made me, you must accept me.

Right?

As usual, there is silence. Hugh breathes into the space below his arms for a while. Gradually, he notices a warm feeling around him, as if someone has turned on the heat.

He says the Lord's Prayer and struggles to his feet.

After the dark church, the basement seems bright, though it's lit only by candles. From across the room, John waves and raises his wine glass.

"Hugh!" he calls over the chatter.

The congregants in the basement have established a vaguely festive scene. On the table are plates of matzoh and dark chocolate, and there are several bottles of wine.

John holds up a bottle. "There's tea and coffee in the kitchen, if you don't drink."

"*In vino veritas.* Wine is good."

"Alternate bites of matzoh and bitter chocolate," John's wife suggests. "It's a sophisticated combination."

Though Hugh might argue with her choice of adjectives, it's a pleasant, warm flavour that goes well with the red wine.

He becomes the focus of attention, peppered with questions, as they admit to being curious about "this piece of fresh meat". He keeps the answers to personal questions short—widower, for a year—and gives more details about his former career and early childhood. There's a young man who picks Hugh's brain about English folk music.

Two glasses of wine later, Hugh is startled when he thinks he hears a distant hand bell.

"Ah. It's time." With a thump of his hand on the table, John pushes himself to his feet. "Bundle up, folks. It's cold out there."

The merriment vanishes as they button their coats and slip on gloves. In silence, they troop up the stairs and out to the garden.

Hugh can make out, at the back, the looming hulk of the crypt and the rows of old, tilting headstones. The sky is a deep, heavy grey with inky clouds that shroud most of the stars. The wind is bitter.

At the front of the yard, in the light of a streetlamp, the minister stands, wrapped in a black wool cloak, a hand bell at her feet.

They bow their heads as she says a short prayer. A soloist sings "Ubi Caritas".

When the minister gives a little nod, Hugh turns to leave but realises everyone else is bending down to the ground. Together, they pick up a long, heavy chain. John moves his hand back and motions to Hugh to take hold.

The metal is cold through the palm of Hugh's glove.

Together, they thread the chain through the handles of the big church door. The minister draws a metal padlock from her pocket and locks the chain with a final clunk.

Hugh feels like he's been hit in the stomach.

John whispers, "It's hard, isn't it? Three days with no Jesus. It's lovely on Sunday when we take the chain off. See you then?"

Hugh nods. He can't speak.

At the car, Hugh takes off a glove and fumbles in his coat pocket for the keys. His breath comes in white puffs.

Just as he opens the door and is about to get in, he hears a gentle voice from no particular direction.

"Thank you for sitting with me."

He freezes, then looks around. Further down the street, a few people are getting into their cars, but there's no one nearby.

With a dry swallow, he whispers to the ground, "You're welcome."

He slides into his seat and drives home.

The light in the front hallway flickers on. In the dimness of the living room, he can see David's urn on the mantelpiece.

Heya, gorgeous. How was it?

Hugh pauses. "Good. It was good. Very good."

Any hot lads?

"Not a one, darling."

Liar.

"I'm shattered. Going to bed now. I love you."

I know. I love you, too.

"I know."

MAP Chat: Nepiophilia

PedoProud: @DontGimmeLolita and @bunnyboy Can I ask both of you a question?

DontGimmeLolita: course

bunnyboy: ya

PedoProud: There's a certain biological logic to hebephilia and ephebophilia, and I can sort of see the various aspects of attraction behind pedophilia.

What's the attraction in nepiophilia, though?

NotHumbert: I've often wondered the same.

What appeals to you @bunnyboy?

bunnyboy: idk theyre just soft and cuddly

theyre so cute

Oskar: What does "idk" mean? I am not familiar with this word. It does not look English.

PedoProud: @Oskar "Idk" stands for "I don't know".

Oskar: Thank you, Pedo Proud.

DontGimmeLolita: Its the same things u like about infants but its stimulating to me

the big eyes and shiny bottom lip that babypowder smell.

Their laugh.

When they throw themselves onto ur lap and just cuddle in

The way everything is either new and so cool like a new toy or even a stick or a rock

Or its the end of the world like a bath or eating a vegetable.

the spectrum I love the spectrum

NotHumbert: Don't you have kids, @DontGimmeLolita? Don't they do the same thing?

DontGimmeLolita: Yeppers

Thats how i figured out exactly what attracts me

When my kids do it it just kicks in the maternal feelings. nothing sexual

When that 6 month old down the street does it it kicks in the heart

bunnyboy: its not like u can fall madly in love with someone who pisses himself though

PedoProud: So it's entirely physical for you, @bunnyboy?

bunnyboy: sure

Oskar: Perhaps, at Bunny Boy's age, he merely has not yet had the opportunity to fall in love.

bunnyboy: im young not dead old man

DontGimmeLolita: okay so we have to do an experiment.

Meet back here in 10 years to see if @bunnyboy's attraction is only physical

26 is old enough to have fallen in love wouldnt u say @Oskar?

NotYourMother: Many people dont have an emotional attraction to others

bunnyboy: i like it when they learn something new

theyre so happy about it

thats kind of a turnon

DontGimmeLolita: Yeah that little rush u get I love that too

And their fat little bellies

PedoProud: Interesting.

Someone should study this.

NotHumbert: They should but I don't think anyone will fund a study on what makes babies sexy.

PedoProud: You'd think they'd want to. The more you know....

Oskar: I agree. I see nothing sexual in an infant. Were I a father, however, I would want to know what might protect my child.

DontGimmeLolita: Me too.

At least i get to know what might be a problem with a nepiophile and my kids

NotYourMother: When god dies and leaves me in charge I'll ensure funding for all the right studies

DontGimmeLolita: Thanks @NotYourMother knew we could count on you

Aaron

April 4, 2017

Dear Ezekiel,

This is one of those letters the person it's written to never gets. Despite the gender problem (It's okay to think of me in a dress. I'm man enough to be okay with that.), I'm a heroine from a classic novel, writing to her dead soldier lover, and I'll burn this letter so only God and the angels know what I've written.

And the Devil, too. Can't forget him.

Why am I writing a letter you'll never get? Because of the news today. It had nothing to do with you. It was just about a teenager who had committed suicide. They said there was no obvious reason for the guy to have killed himself because he was a grade-A student and he had a girlfriend and he wasn't bullied that anyone knew of. As if those were the only reasons to kill yourself.

I think the main reason people kill themselves is because they think no one loves them.

At some point in your life, you'll probably feel like no one loves you. Not so.

Along with the usual mother/father/grandparents/brother and sister/friends/other people you've impressed along the way, I loved you. A lot.

I never want you to feel like no one loves you. I don't care what your grades are or who you're having sex (or not having sex) with. Never kill yourself.

While I'm giving orders, never hurt yourself, never hurt others on purpose, and don't forget to brush your teeth. I'm starting to feel like an old man, so I can say these things.

I loved you.

I love you.

At least, I love the memory of you. I haven't seen you in 15 years, 4 months and 21 days. I don't know for sure if I would still love you, but I think I would. I don't know if you'd still love me.

We used to love each other.

Are you doing the math in your head now? Yeah, you were only 11 months old when we met. Actually, you weren't even quite 11 months. I was 16. Your parents needed a babysitter for a few days a week after school and sometimes in the evening so they could go out. It was kind of funny because your dad was the one who didn't want to leave you. Your mom had to haul him out by the arm, every time. For every text I got from your mom, I got 8 from your dad. As I'm sure you know by now, he's the kind of guy who worried about your temperature and the texture of your clothes and how many milligrams of vitamin C you got every day. Your mom, back then, was a little more chill. She said parenting included letting you fall down a couple of times so you learned how to pick yourself up. Your mom and dad actually once argued in front of me because she let you eat something without washing your hands first.

Anyway, I knew from talking to your dad on the phone that he was the one I'd have to wow during the interview. You were asleep when I arrived, so I spent a little over an hour sitting on the deep red carpet in your jade green living room, being grilled about what I would do in certain situations.

I'd had a lot of babysitting experience by then, and even his crazy "hypothetical" questions had pretty obvious answers. Guess I passed his test, because he eventually left me alone with your mom and went to get you.

When you were brought into the room, you weren't even a little bit shy, even though you'd just woken up. Your wispy hair was still kind of stuck to your pink cheek, and your thumb was still stuck in your mouth, but you looked at me like I was a new toy—something to investigate. You couldn't walk more than a couple of steps, but you scrambled off your dad's lap and made your way over to me by holding on to the furniture.

I think I said, "Hi." I held a finger out to you, and you took it. You stared at me for almost a minute. Your eyes were a deep, steely blue.

That minute was harder than passing your dad's test, but I guess I passed yours, too. I picked up a board book from the pile on the coffee table, and you flumped down on your little ass, sucking your thumb while I turned the book to read it to you. When that book was done, you grabbed another book from the pile and flumped down on my lap. Your thumb went straight back in your mouth.

That was the best feeling I've ever had. No one has ever scrutinised me like that and then accepted me.

I wonder if that guy who committed suicide ever felt that. Probably not. Feeling that just once is enough to get me through my lifetime, I think.

Two days later was a Saturday, and we got to stay alone together for an hour. It was another of your dad's tests. He had lined up age-appropriate educational toys on the dining room table, in order of your preference. He had prepared your snack and left a bottle of breast milk in the fridge, with the warming instructions printed out and posted on the door. He left three pages of things to do when you cried.

You didn't do that. You didn't cry even when your parents went out the door. You looked at me and, with that stare of yours, said, "Prove yourself."

"Okay. What would you like to do?" I asked.

You hid behind the sofa, peeking at me around the corner. I did what any good opponent would do. I got down on my hands and knees, hid around the other corner and squeaked like a mouse until you found me. We played hunt-and-chase around the sofa for almost 15 minutes. You were really only interested in being the hunter, so I remained a mouse the whole time.

Then we examined the pattern on the carpet for a while, naming the colours. You pointed to things around the room, demanding I tell you the name.

"Dis!"

"That's a chair."

"Dis!"

"That's a clock."

"Dis!"

"That's a fern."

Then you held my finger and we walked into the kitchen together. On the way through, I thought to mess up the toys on the dining room table, so it would look like we followed instructions.

When your parents came home, 10 minutes early, you were sitting on my lap while I read to you. You absent-mindedly picked tiny cubes of soft cheese and peaches from the dish in my right hand, noshing like you were eating popcorn at a movie.

Your dad asked question after question about what we'd done in the 50 minutes, but your mom interrupted to ask if I could stay for another hour.

"I'll pay you for the extra time and throw in 5 bucks more. It was really nice to have some adult time, and he seems happy with you."

Your dad looked like she'd grown three heads.

"No problem," I said.

"We'll just be at the coffee shop on the corner," she sighed, relieved. "If you could get him ready for bed, that would be great. There are pyjamas in the top drawer of his dresser." She literally yanked your dad back out the door, with him glancing at me suspiciously and kind of sputtering at your mom.

"No problem."

You watched them go and then slapped the book with an open palm. "Dis."

"Okay. Do you want more peach?"

You grabbed the empty dish by its edge and held it up to my face. "Dis."

You understood every word I said.

By the time they returned again, you were lazing in my arms, giving off that awesome baby smell in your clean sleepers, your small hands wrapped around the last of the bottle of milk.

I guess I passed everyone's test. Answering your dad's 7 texts was probably a good idea. He officially hired me before I left the house.

That was in the very early autumn, when the weather was still like summer. We spent at least 6 hours per week together, but usually a little more because your mother was pretty interested in going out on the weekends.

Wait, don't get me wrong. It's not like your dad loved you and your mom wanted to be away from you. They just had different ways of showing their love. Your mom, I think, had nothing to prove. She was from a big family, she said, and it seemed like she was used to having lots of people raise a kid. Your dad never talked about his family, but your mom once mentioned that he was raised by a single mom. I think she muttered "overcompensating" under her breath, but I couldn't be sure.

I don't have kids so, even though I liked your mom's style, I can't say which way was actually better. In a way, I understood your dad more. Like him, I watched your every move, noticed every change. I tried to make everything perfect for you. If you were still napping when I arrived, I liked to spend the time making a special arrangement of toys or a fancy snack for you. You liked things that looked good. You'd smack both hands against your little cheeks and go, "Ohhhhhhh!" It was worth the effort, every time. I had gone to the library and found a book about making good kid food. You loved the organic apple pancakes that I made in Mickey Mouse shapes. You loved the blanket forts, and the mini water park I set up in the kitchen one rainy day. You loved the big cardboard box I brought (though your dad was a little worried about germs and wanted something washable, but your mom put her foot down).

In October, your parents bought a trampoline for the back yard. It was an adult trampoline, intended to provide an entertaining cardio workout for your mother,

195

who wanted her pre-you body back. You loved the trampoline—but, of course, your father was concerned about whiplash.

Your mom and I took you on it anyway.

I would sit cross-legged, holding your hands until your small body became used to the wobbly terrain. Over a few weeks, your body strengthened. Your jumps became surer, more controlled. You discovered that, if you jumped beside me as I sat, you could make me bounce a little.

"Dis!" You pointed at my hair, captivated by the idea that your jumping made it flop.

There was no laughter when you bounced me. It was a serious scientific experiment, and I watched your furrowed brow and intense eyes with fascination.

I knew I loved you.

Your father slowly became proud of our relationship. He loved the way we responded to each other, the way I could predict your needs, teach you things. He admitted it was good that I knew when to help

196

you and when to let you fail. We talked about that when you were learning to use a crayon. Your dad kept his hand over yours, forcing the accurate lines and identifiable shapes to remain on the paper; I put some newspaper underneath and let you mangle a few crayons.

"It's good for him to mess up a little and break things," I told your dad as he reached over to help you. "It's creating stronger neural pathway in the brain."

He was impressed with my Psych 101.

"I guess that's true," he acknowledged, "but it's instinct for me to protect him and teach him."

"Instinct is good." I let him have that.

He always bragged to his friends about how smart you were, and how good we were together, how I encouraged your development. A couple of people asked if I could babysit their kids, too, but I said my schedule was pretty full, what with school and taking care of you.

I wasn't lying. Even my friends said I never had time to hang out with them anymore. I was either with you, doing schoolwork or sleeping. They said I was like a dad—boring, like a dad.

You grew so quickly. You could walk by yourself and climb into chairs by yourself. You started talking. You were "Zee-el" and I was "Awon". Very rarely did you want "Awon do." Most of the time it was "Zee-el do!" "Zee-el" did his own feeding and his own colouring, and he put his own clothes on... kind of. "Zee-el" knew all the colours in the wooden puzzles, and the names of the animals on the educational game that had blinky lights and animal sounds. Your parents showed you off to their friends and relatives, and your dad liked to do surreptitious demonstrations in the park when there just happened to be a lot of parents close by.

There was one thing you would do only for me, though, and that was to give a special hug. You would curl up in my lap, your head resting on my left collarbone, and pat my right collarbone. I would wrap both arms around you. We would rock gently.

This was our signature hug. It didn't require kisses or declarations of love. It didn't elicit smiles or laughter. It never turned into a tickle war. It was a simple expression of how we felt about each other.

You hugged your parents, too—you were an affectionate kid, and I hope that stayed as you grew. The affection you showed other people was pleasant and youthful and a brilliant spark in the moment; the affection we showed each other was deep and solid.

You learned to play with words. Attempting to multitask, I would review my class notes orally while changing you or feeding you fresh pear and milk-softened squares of shredded wheat. Just before a history test, I was explaining the creation of the country, and you giggled whenever I said *confederation*. The more I repeated the word, the more I was rewarded.

"Con-fed-er-a-*tion*!"

You laughed so hard you had to rest your head on your food-smeared sweatshirt sleeve.

It became the amusement of the week. Without cause, you would look at me slyly, a sideways glance of duplicity.

"Cun."

"Con," I would repeat.

"Fud.

"Fed."

"Ew."

"Er."

"AYSHUM!"

I would use the last two syllables as an excuse to tickle you.

Finally, exhausted by your own humour, you would collapse, spread-eagled, on the floor.

"You're funny, Ezekiel."

"Yu sunny."

"No, *you're* funny."

We were so good together—but maybe a little too good. Finally, after weeks of them asking, I went to hang with a couple of my friends. We were playing FIFA in my friend's bedroom, and the other two were talking about their girlfriends. They noticed my silence before I did.

"Aaron, you got a girlfriend yet?"

"Nah. Too busy for one of those." I remember staring at the game screen, suddenly aware that I just didn't want to have that discussion.

"You gotta get a life," one of them said.

The guy who was supposed to be my best friend threw the biggest stone first. "He's getting lots of little boy dick."

I did the only thing I could. I kept on playing the video game. "That's fucking disgusting. You should kill yourself for even saying things like that, asshole."

There was an awkward silence. I didn't want to see if they were looking at each other. Eventually, we all returned to the game and pretended we'd never been talking about sex.

What he said stayed with me, at the back of my mind. It ate like a worm at the time we spent together. It started gnawing at our special hug, our exchanged glances.

You started looking at me as though I'd said something hurtful.

Did I want you that way? I don't know. I never really thought about you like that, but I was timid of your body. When changing or bathing you, I used a discretion that was absolutely Victorian, keeping my gaze averted and using a thick washcloth, keeping you covered whenever possible. I sided with your dad when your mother suggested that we let you run around naked to encourage toilet training.

I gave my notice to your dad a little while later. I said I just had too much schoolwork to make the time commitment you guys needed.

I didn't cry the last time I left you. I don't know if you cried. I never talked to anyone in your family again.

I know now what I am. I've known for a long time, maybe even since before I met you. I've come to terms with it. For a while, I tried to stay away from kids, but it turns out I didn't need to. I trained as an ECE teacher, and I'm a really good one, too. I work in schools, where there are always large groups and other adults.

No one else knows. No one has even suspected.

I've fallen for a couple of other kids, but you were the special one. When they say there's only one soulmate for each of us, I believe them, I think. I have never found anyone, child or adult, who made me feel the way you did.

Could it have hurt you if I'd stayed? Maybe. I think I loved you too much to keep my distance. Though I would never have abused you, at some point I would have let a look linger too long or said something too familiar. Someone would have figured it out and, even if I had never touched you, they would be suspicious. Forever, people would think "Poor Zeke", and everything you did would have been put in context of the abuse they were sure you'd suffered.

I know now that some people like me can be with people like you, but I didn't want to take that chance. For me, it was better to let you go than risk it.

I'm going to burn this letter now. As it goes up in smoke, it'll go with a prayer for you.

Remember, always, that you were loved.

Yours, Aaron

MAP Chat: Limerence

PedoProud: I am sooooo wired today :) :) :)

NotHumbert: What's up?

DontGimmeLolita: Uh oh

Someones in love

PedoProud: *blush*

bunnyboy: an adult

PedoProud: A classmate's kid.

NotHumbert: That's nice.

DontGimmeLolita: details

PedoProud: We're working on a group project, but she's got two kids, so we do the work at her place.

Oskar: How old are the children?

PedoProud: The baby is, like, two. The girl is twelve. My classmate had her young.

bunnyboy: so u have to babysit

PedoProud: No. Her partner took the baby, but the girl stayed with us because she wanted to learn about what we were doing.

bunnyboy: boring

PedoProud: A 12-year-old can learn gender studies. It's not boring.

DontGimmeLolita: And u just mooned all evening

      Butterflies in ur belly and ur heart skipping

PedoProud: She was so into it! She asked me all these great questions! Like, she made me think so hard sometimes.

      It was incredibly awesome.

      Yeah, @DontGimmeLolita, all of that stuff....

DontGimmeLolita: the high of new love

Oskar: The limerence follows.

DontGimmeLolita: and then the crash.

bunnyboy: whats limerence

NotHumbert: Thats what anti-contacts get in place of love.

Oskar: It is an obsession that is born out of unrequited love. It is common for people like us.

PedoProud: You guys are really harshing my buzz here.

NotHumbert: Will you see her again?

PedoProud: Probably. We'll need another meeting or two.

DontGimmeLolita: And then never to see her again

PedoProud: I am so totally not listening to you. *Puts her hands over her ears* La, la, la, la!

DontGimmeLolita: Go ahead.

Tell us all about her

PedoProud: She's got this really gorgeous skin and totally sick brown eyes, and every time she's confused about something her little mouth twists to the side and she gets a little wrinkle between her eyes and she's so smart!

DontGimmeLolita: She sounds awesome

bunnyboy: so shouldnt you stay away from her

NotYourMother: Not all MAPs see the need to avoid children

PedoProud: I never need to avoid them. I have free will.

Besides, it's an emotional attraction, not a physical one.

bunnyboy: im never gonna fall in love

im never gonna have limerence

NotYourMother: Place your bets here

Marie

At 2:50 p.m. Marie puts the kettle on. The tea set has been waiting on the tray since just after lunch. There is no cream, but he doesn't take cream, so she will be the only one to suffer.

As the kettle boils, she arranges homemade cinnamon cookies on a small plate and pulls two fresh linen napkins from the top drawer of the buffet. The sink is piled with her lunch dishes and baking equipment; she briefly considers washing them but dismisses the idea. It will give him something to complain about, she tells herself.

She chose him out of three contenders, just over four years ago. The other two were perfectly acceptable readers—clear voices, good diction—but she was intrigued by the scent of earthy, exotic cooking that rose from his clothes, and by his accent. She imagines his tongue to be a dual creature: a lithe and agile little rodent at the tip, and a majestic, unhurried elephant at the back. His lips must also be thick, as his *m*'s and *b*'s have a leisurely air to them.

The doorbell rings. She feels for his envelope on the hall table; he prefers to surreptitiously pick it up on his way out the door. She used to, in the beginning, hand the envelope to him, but his embarrassment was hard on them both.

"Madame Marie."

"What's wrong, Alphonse? You sound like you're ill."

"A cold, Madame Marie. Just a small-small cold."

"Oh, well. Are you sure you're up for this?"

"If you allow me in de door, yes."

"Of course. Sorry...." She steps back to let him in.

He sits on the chair to remove laced-up, hard leather shoes, and replaces them with slippers that clop when he walks on a bit of bare floor.

"Madame, your maid has neglected to come again." It is, as usual, not phrased as a question.

"Dear Alphonse, if she has not come in the approximately forty years since my children grew up, we cannot continue to hold it against her, can we?"

"I am merely concerned for your comfort. If you would ever need me to assist wit' dusting, I would be pleased to offer my services."

"Stick with your day job, sir. I will not condone the murder of all my dust-bunny companions. Simon, for instance," she says, indicating to the corner behind the hall table, "would be a great loss."

She hears him snort with laughter, and this is followed by a short, harsh cough.

"You have pointed to somet'ing de size of an animal, Madame." He coughs again.

"I figured as much. The way the air flows in this area, dust would find a safe home in that corner." She calls over her shoulder as she returns to the kitchen. "I give you permission to do away with Simon—and *only* Simon. Do not move things around on me."

She empties the boiled kettle into the teapot. He comes into the kitchen, and she hears the lid to the garbage bin open and shut.

"May I carry de tray for you?"

"No, thank you. Would you like honey in your tea? It might be good for your throat."

"Perhaps."

"It's in the cupboard beside the fridge. You could bring that to the sitting room. The tea tray is too full."

"Too full? It seems to be missing de cream pitcher."

"I was too busy to go shopping. It's of no concern to you, unless you've changed your preferences over the last week."

They assume their customary seats. His bag, when he places it on the floor, thunks more heavily than usual.

"What's in the bag?"

He clears his throat. "A series of poetry pamphlets—*chapbooks*, I believe de woman called dem. Dey are by a young Australian poet. I also purchased an old copy of *To Kill a Mockingbird*."

"I got that on Audible ages ago." She frowns.

"It is for myself."

"Lovely. How old? May I see?"

He lays the book in her upturned hands.

"De dust jacket is black, orange and green. De title is at de top. Dere is a tree on de bottom part."

"Their communication tree. I think I remember the cover from when it first came out. Is this a first edition?" Her hands brush the fragile paper cover, smooth over the coarse inner pages. Bringing the book to her nose, she inhales. "Oh, that's marvelous."

Reluctantly, she hands it back.

Between sips of tea, they each relate events of their week. Marie has recently noticed the dwindling length of this topic of conversation. The death of Alphonse's son, just six months ago, seemed to provoke a deliberate retreat from unnecessary activity. He draws out a simple church service to make it seem like a day at the races. She compensates by describing a music lecture in detail.

"But dat is enough of de social gossip. What shall we read?"

She has forgotten he has no interest in European classical music. "Either the Irish history or the new poetry."

She hears him riffling through his bag. "I do not understand de attraction to dat history."

"That's because you lack a fundamental appreciation of juxtaposition, Alphonse. Your accent and the Irish gift of the gab sound lovely together."

"I t'ink you are merely a sadist. You like to see suffering."

"I never denied your company brings me pleasure."

He coughs, and she can't tell if he's smiling. His teacup clinks against its saucer. A couple of pages turn, and his voice rasps across the room to her.

It's only ten minutes before his voice begins to give out. He breaks into a cough.

Disappointment, almost crushing, seeps down her chest. "Though it saddens me to say this, I think we'd better postpone this reading. Your voice just isn't up for it today."

He sips some tea. "I agree de aest'etics are not good. I apologise. I did not realise de quantity of amphibians I am dealing wit'."

"Not at all. Maybe some lemon along with the honey would help?"

She brings lemon slices from the kitchen and pours him a hot cup. "Would you like to listen to music instead?"

"Or you could tell me a story. Are you good at telling stories, Madame?"

"I can't say I've told too many stories since my children were small."

"You have heard so many. You must be able to tell one."

"And what should this story be about?"

"Love, of course. Dat is do only t'ing we tell stories about: de love of a person, de love of a t'ing we do, de love of an idea...."

"Love, it is, then." She assembles a napkin of cookies and refreshes her own cup. Turning her face towards his chair, she contemplates for a moment. "Once upon a time—"

He chortles quietly.

"Do not laugh at the storyteller, or the storyteller may have her revenge. She is the one with the power."

"I apologise. Continue, please."

"Once upon a time, there was a young woman just coming to marriageable age. This woman was beginning to be a little troublesome to her parents: the university dream had been successfully quashed by the reality of finances, and the young woman was not doing what she ought to have been doing when it came to learning short-hand and practising telephone etiquette. She did insist on reading every book in the public library, as well as shamelessly befriending the owner of the local bookstore who was not, contrary to what the town believed, solely interested in Harlequin Romances and golf books. No, this bookstore owner had a little side business running out of his back room that included a 1908 copy of G.H. Hardy's *Course in Pure Mathematics* and a lovely new book from someone named Alfred Kinsey."

"Dis is not fiction, I see."

"Shh, Alphonse. Drink your tea.

"Well, the only thing to do with such a woman is to marry her off to anyone who will agree to have her. An appropriate gentleman was sought, found and accepted, as the woman was growing tired of all the conflict and figured married life couldn't be any worse than unmarried life.

"The summer before she was to be married, she took a short bus ride and a not-too-long train ride to a lovely old house—an estate, really, out in the country. There, she was one of three young people hired to help out a mother whose seven children were home from private boarding school for the summer.

"The young woman's job was to prepare food for the children and take care of their things: clean their rooms, wash their clothes, purchase the paper and pencils required by the private tutor and the educational toys required by the nanny.

"Once the young woman learned to cut bologna sandwiches on the diagonal and chicken salad sandwiches into squares, most of the training was finished. It was not a terribly demanding job, though she liked the children well-enough. Her own lunch hours, after the aquamarine Melmac plates had been washed, were spent reading in the garden.

"About two weeks into the job, the young woman ran out of reading material. It was a Tuesday. She wouldn't have time off until the following Saturday afternoon. Forlornly, she sat on a white cast-iron chair to reread one of the books she had brought with her.

"A shadow fell over her. His—no, let us maintain a certain air of mystery and call him 'L'—L stood in front of her and said, 'You've already read that one. I think rereading a book is really boring.'

"L was thin and wiry, of average height but tow-headed, so he seemed a little taller than he actually was. He was quick-witted, intelligent, and had intense eyes that seemed to pierce space. When she explained the situation, he awkwardly reached out to pluck her sleeve. 'Come with me. There's a library in the attic.'

"Indeed, there was a library. It was a good size, perhaps almost a thousand books, mildewing away on old wooden shelves under damp eaves. Some of the books were quite old; it looked as though nothing had been added to the collection for twenty years or more.

"The young woman reached out to take a book, but L stopped her with a raised palm. 'Wait. May I choose one for you?'

"Though they had been acquainted for a mere two weeks, the woman was titillated by the idea that he would consider suggesting this, and she agreed. Placing his fingertips on the book spines, he began to walk slowly in front of the shelves, watching her face, her eyes.

"There was a microsecond of magic: would L be able to choose a book for her? He had clearly been studying her, keeping track of what she did. Perhaps they had some mystic connection? No, of course not. Her eyes widened as he passed over a copy of the third edition of Hardy's *Pure Mathematics*; his nimble fingers plucked it from the shelf.

"'You are amazing.' They laughed at his magic trick.

"'Taught by the best of the best. Do you understand everything in this book?'

"'Not yet.'

"'I'm not very good at math, but I like it. Teach me what you do know.'

"'In exchange for you teaching me something.'

"His eyes cast about the room. 'I'm good at juggling.'

"'Groovy.'

"In the late evening, when the younger children had been put to bed and the older ones were left to their own devices, the young woman and L sat at the kitchen table, under the low orange hanging lamp, as moths beat at the screen window. With a spiral-bound notebook for each of them, and the text between them, they pored over the pages, watching the numbers blossom into elegant order. When they got to a section the woman didn't understand, L looked disheartened, as if he were missing a party. She would spend the next couple of days frantically working through it, just so she could see the delight on his face when he came to be intimate with integers and De Moivre's Theorem and discontinuous functions.

"With the discovery of the book, they began an intense friendship. There was no slow build-up or gradual realisation; it was the sudden click of mutual understanding that translated into lunch hours of magic tricks and evenings of Hardy's mathematics. Sometimes, they would read to each other from the musty children's books from the attic library.

"There was very little that didn't interest L. He would perch on a Naugahyde bar stool at the end of the kitchen counter, lean on his elbows and talk with her while she prepared baked beans and butter-fried wieners. He bombarded her with questions like a small child, and he followed each of her answers with another 'Why?' When she said it was his turn to entertain her, he told stories of the children playing, and he could imitate their voices perfectly, mimic their hand movements—but would then become self-conscious when she praised the skill, insisting he wasn't trying to mock anyone.

"The young woman was wounded by causing discomfort when she meant to praise. She conscientiously worked around his insecurity, learned to offer compliments he was able to accept. Never once did she do anything as base as stroke his male ego, but she made sure he knew when she was amused or pleased by something he said or did. As L became more confident around her, he returned the sincerity. In their few minutes together each day, escaping ordinary life, they were able to relax and refresh themselves.

"L's birthday, she discovered, was in the middle of July.

"'What would you like for your birthday?' she asked, one afternoon as he watched her fold laundry. Immediately, she realised she wouldn't be able to buy him a good present, so she added, 'I could make you a cake, if you like.'

"His eyes lit up. 'A really big cake.' His hands described a tower from his waist to his forehead. 'I've never had a super tall cake. They're always flat and one layer. They're so disappointing. I want something fit for a king.'

"So the young woman received permission from the lady of the house, and she bought fresh ingredients. She made two angel food cakes in tube pans, and sliced the cakes into layers. Between the layers, she smeared thick whipped cream and arranged whole Gariguette strawberries. On top of the cake, she stuck a blue birthday candle for every year.

"The cake was so tall it couldn't be sliced in the normal way. The family gathered, and they all scooped chunks from the tower into bowls, with the children cackling and licking cream from their fingers. They drank lemon-lime soda with it.

"The recompense for all her effort was the grin he gave her over the top of his bowl.

"For the rest of the summer, the children talked of L and his birthday cake as though it were a hero's quest. L, of course, didn't try to stop them. He may even have been the one to increase the height of the tower cake with each telling. The woman would smile shyly, and never once insisted he tell the truth.

"One sleepy Sunday afternoon, he led her through a field and down a path to a creek.

"'Take off your sandals,' he insisted. 'It's best without shoes.'

"They hopped across the flat rocks in the stream, spied on drowsing crayfish, and dragged their fingers through the long algae that L said was the hair of mermaids. L picked up a worm and wiggled it in front of her face, waiting for her to scream; she countered with a flying gob of wet silt that elicited a squawk from him. They splashed each other until rivulets of cool water ran down their faces.

"When they left the stream, L gallantly held out a hand to help her up the bank.

"Toward the end of the summer, their talks became more personal. They could complain to each other about the dullness of a day, and how unfair parental expectations could be. They talked of dreams and unattainable futures without ever falling into pessimism. L confessed his dream of becoming a race-car driver, though he knew he was too academic, too much of a 'nerd' for that to happen. The woman had no real, concrete dreams but, when pressed, she admitted she would like to become a librarian in a university library. L used his fingers to make goggle-like glasses around his eyes, and he tiptoed around the backyard, pretending to hiss at imaginary people who were making too much noise as they read their books.

"Of course, they eventually had to go their separate ways. The summer ended, as it always does. On the night before the young woman was to return home, the family had a celebratory barbecue. L gave her a going-away gift of a new copy of *Charlotte's Web*. Over the platters of burgers and spare ribs, L and the woman stole glances at each other,

223

giggled nervously, and later parted with a single quick, awkward embrace.

"The young woman went home, became officially immersed in wedding plans, and married the nice young man who had a perfectly respectable job and a perfectly respectable position in their small town. The husband was kind, gentle and over all a nice man. Throughout the first year of the marriage, until the first baby arrived, the young woman was bolstered by letters from L. Eventually, though, the letters slowed and then stopped. She was worried her husband would find one of the letters, so, after committing them to memory, she burned them and kept everything as a book in her mind.

"She thought of L every night, as she fell asleep, even when she was in her husband's arms. As each of her children grew up and moved away, and when her husband died, she comforted herself by reading her mental book of letters."

Marie stops speaking abruptly. She sighs and takes a bite of her cookie.

Alphonse's cup rattles a little as he takes a sip of tea. "Dat is a heartbreaking story about compromise."

She shrugs. "Or a realistic story about love."

"No, dat is pain, pure pain, Madame. I was so very lucky to marry de woman I loved wit' all my heart and soul. I never one time t'ought about someone who was not her. Never one time."

"You've never spoken much about her. Next time, when your voice is better, you'll have to tell me about her."

As Alphonse leaves, he pauses, as usual, at the hall table, but she doesn't hear the swish of paper against wood. When she checks, the envelope has been left where she placed it.

She takes the tea tray to the kitchen and adds the dirty cups to the pile of dishes in the sink.

The emptiness of the afternoon is loud around her. She has a sudden longing for strawberry angel food cake.

Though she knows the imported winter berries will not taste the same, she puts on her coat, and picks up her white cane and shopping bag. As she has no companion with her, she will have to ask a salesclerk to help

225

her select twelve small blue candles for the
top of the cake.

MAP Chat: Pedo Hunters

bunnyboy: hey6

ChatBot: I'm sorry. The chat room is empty. Please try again later.

bunnyboy: guys

ChatBot: I'm sorry. The chat room is empty. Please try again later.

bunnyboy: fuck off bot

     guys

NotYourMother: Sup @bunnyboy

bunnyboy: ...

NotYourMother: Are you okay.

bunnyboy: no

NotYourMother: What happened.

bunnyboy: i got a death threat

     i ignored it

     they tried to dox me

     but they got the wrong guy

NotYourMother: Hold on. Hold on

Let me get some of the others.

bunnyboy: im not going anywhere

nowhere to go

NotYourMother: Tell me everything

bunnyboy: nothing else to tell

Oskar: How did they get the wrong person?

bunnyboy: they're fucking stupid

PedoProud: How did they get your information?

bunnyboy: dunno

they didnt get it all

no picture

NotYourMother: What did they get?

bunnyboy: city

school

street

first name

NotHumbert: What do you mean "they got the wrong guy"

bunnyboy: my classmate

228

we live on the same street

we have the same first name

NotHumbert: You've gotta tell the police,
@bunnyboy

bunnyboy: they know

they told me

he's dead

NotHumbert: shit

PedoProud: Oh my god.

Oskar: You have taken precautions, Bunny
Boy? You are safe?

bunnyboy: they arrested them

DontGimmeLolita: shit

if you lived close to me @bunnyboy I
would hold you tight and never let you go

bunnyboy: if you lived close

id let you

Josh

When his head hits the cement, he's aware of a slushy sound similar to when he and his best friend smashed the Halloween pumpkin on the sidewalk; at the same time, there's a crack that sounds distant.

Before the pain starts, he thinks, Oh. At least we've got there. No more waiting. This is it.

Because the waiting was a total... what's the word? Drag? Pain in the ass? No, not strong enough. The unnameable stress to waiting for something, a long ice pick incessantly chipping through his chest, and now the relief of the wait finally being over is cool, like cucumber water in a thin crystal glass.

It was just a few minutes between when he'd first realised there was someone behind him and when he knew they were going to hurt him. Why? Why were they going to hurt him? They couldn't possibly know. He'd never told anyone, never written it down. Perhaps they were trying to rob him. He's not some martyr-type who would try to fight off the thugs just to save his iPod and a mostly-empty wallet, so he held out the backpack. Someone tore it from his hand, but they didn't show any interest in it. Their hands grabbed straight for his t-shirt, his hair, his throat.

The pain hits like a wall of sound, shaking every atom in his body.

As he becomes aware of the pain on the left side of his skull, which radiates to the back and right side before circling around to his forehead, more pain spikes him, first in his stomach and then his lower spine.

Boots.

He hadn't noticed that they were wearing boots. Odd, he thinks, given the heat. Everyone else on the street is wearing the least amount of footwear possible: sandals, flip-flops. Even the diehards wear light canvas sneakers. There was the lady by the beer store who had kicked off her pink kitten-heeled slippers and was walking barefoot along the sidewalk. He should have noticed the big, ankle-covering, lace-up boots with thick treads—should have heard the clomping and stomping. They wouldn't have sounded normal now. Only in the winter. If it had been winter, he could have been wearing a puffy coat with a fur-lined hood, and maybe some of the blood would have been absorbed by the coat. Certainly, it would have offered a little protection from the boots...

Heat sears his right kidney. They have fire? No, the heat is from inside. It bursts from a spot just beneath the skin, burning his lower back, forcing him to turn, exposing his stomach. Quickly, though, the force of the vomiting spins him on his side again.

There's an explosion in front of his face. Just another kick: the light is behind his eyes. He can't breathe through his nose, like it's just suddenly not there anymore. Where it used to be is only a mess of loose flesh.

Blood tastes gross. There's an aura of meat—rich in iron and protein—but the cloying of it at the back of his throat makes him gag again. He tries to push some of it out of his mouth with his tongue.

All he wants is one good, clear breath. His ribs heave, but he's only getting sips of useable oxygen. What happened to the air? Has someone sprayed a chemical—a poison? The boot owners don't seem to notice it.

One of them grabs a fistful of his hair and smashes his skull on the pavement again.

He falls, gratefully, through blackness.

MAP Chat: Acceptable Outlets

bunnyboy: been doing research

why is canada a bad country

DontGimmeLolita: no Cadbury Flaky

NotHumbert: Prejudice.

PedoProud: Post-colonialism and the consequent treatment of minorities.

bunnyboy: bzzzzzzt wrong

porn laws

DontGimmeLolita: Whats wrong with them

bunnyboy: everythings banned

no drawings no stories no dolls nothing

DontGimmeLolita: All their porn?

bunnyboy: nah

u can get really graphic adult stuff

scary adult stuff both real and drawn

just no kids

not even anime

NotHumbert: Ahh, the good old ick factor.

It's disgusting so let's ban it, even if it doesn't involve a real person.

Logic doesn't play into it.

They should leave us the hentai and go after the countries that still allow real CP.

Oskar: I agree with the total ban. Even drawings can be the beginning of a problem.

PedoProud: How so, @Oskar?

Oskar: We must protect the children.

NotHumbert: I disagree.

You ever think about stuff? Fantasies?

Oskar: Of course.

NotHumbert: What's the difference?

You want to protect the poor, innocent paper from bad words and offensive images?

Oskar: You are being ridiculous. I am protecting children. Pornography is... how do you call it? A gateway drug. If one starts with pictures and words, one will soon need more intense stimulation. One will soon turn to live pornography.

PedoProud: I'm okay with stories and drawings. I draw my line at real images. I

235

don't even want images that look like real kids.

I love hentai, though. Love it so much.

DontGimmeLolita: Id die without hentai

NotHumbert: Hentai's weird.

Weird 2D squished up faces.

They're deformed. Not a turn-on.

DontGimmeLolita: Ive got myself so well-trained to lolis and shotas that 3D doesnt do it for me.

NotHumbert: @DontGimmeLolita Well that's just weird in itself.

bunnyboy: sick kink

NotHumbert: I like stories. I write them for myself.

PedoProud: @NotHumbert You do?

NotHumbert: Yep.

By hand on paper.

PedoProud: Do you keep a book?

NotHumbert: Sometimes I get paranoid and destroy them, but I usually have 2 or 3 on hand to choose from.

bunnyboy: kiddie porn is still legal in parts of the world

    and theres thailand

NotYourMother: Treading the fine line

bunnyboy: i didnt say it was good

    im never gonna use it

    just stating facts

<u>Ivan</u>

The bell that sets them free from class rang fifteen minutes ago; the bell that tells them they should be either at after-school activities or off school property is about to ring.

Ivan leans against the bank of lockers and rests a hand on Lin's hip. He likes the texture of her summer dress, the corrugated feel of the gathered cotton where the skirt meets the waist. As Lin moves, the flowered fabric swishes against the thigh of his black jeans.

He catches her eye and grins.

She kisses him and gives him the half-smile that makes his chest all warm. "What homework do we have again?"

Her thick, straight, black hair slips easily between his fingers. "Give me another kiss and I'll tell you."

She obliges.

"Read Chapter Seven and do the questions for history, and..."

"And?"

His lips purse: she kisses him again.

"Come up with a theme for your visual arts project, and..."

She takes his face in both hands, bringing his lips within millimetres of hers. "Tell me, and then you can have your kiss."

"Nuh-uh. Payment first."

Without moving away from Ivan, Lin bellows, "Jia-Ling! What's for chemistry homework?"

"Got none tonight!"

Lin raises an eyebrow at Ivan, pats his cheek and takes a step backwards.

The bell shrieks, but the crowd doesn't seem to acknowledge it.

"Not working tonight?" She hikes up her backpack to free a few strands of hair from beneath the strap.

"Nope. Home—and home alone, too, I hope."

"Lucky. I'm on 'til ten."

"Shit. Breakfast homework again?"

"You betcha. Gotta go." She stands on her toes for a last kiss.

Teachers scuttle along the hallway, shooing students outside. There's a guffaw and a groan as the math teacher threatens more homework. Ivan bumps fists with his friends as they walk out of the school.

With both earbuds firmly in, he scrolls through his iPod to find a playlist he has entitled F.I.A. Neutral Milk Hotel jolts through his ears.

Buses and vans zoom past him in the diamond lane, blowing dust in whorls against his back. He can feel the grains of sand lightly stinging the bare skin of his arm, below the sleeve of his black t-shirt. The sun is hot; his feet sweat inside his high tops.

To Ivan's disdain, his family lives in an ordinary suburban bungalow in an ordinary suburban neighbourhood. Chosen for its tranquility and distance from busy roads, the beige brick house boasts nothing more interesting than a few nice maple trees and a lot of lawn that requires regular mowing. When Ivan's mother remarried ten years ago and the family moved here, Ivan was not bothered by the placidness of the environment; now, he counts the days until he leaves for university.

The house is still quiet. The bus that delivers his brother will be another fifteen minutes. In an hour, his half-sister and stepfather will come crashing in, and the chaos will begin: do this, do that, what's this, could you please? His mother will arrive home last, arms overloaded with briefcases and zippered leather binders.

Immediately inside the door, Ivan whips off his shoes and socks and strides along the wooden hallway in his bare feet. The room he shares with his brother is at the back of the house. There, he flings his footwear on the floor and his backpack on the army-green blanket that lies rumpled on the mattress.

On the other side of the room, Dmitri's immaculate bed and tidy desk glare accusingly.

Ivan strips off his sweaty black jeans, tosses them on top of his discarded shoes and replaces them with black cut-offs. He musses his shoulder-length blue hair and checks the mirror to make sure he hasn't lost any earrings throughout the day.

With the windows open, the house is cool. He can hear the afternoon sounds of the neighbourhood: school buses, voices, dogs, basketballs and, in the background, birds in the newly-leafy trees.

Ravenous, he heads to the kitchen.

The screen door slams just as Ivan is balancing his massive sandwich, glass of milk and bowl of ice cream on one arm.

"Did you make one for me?" Dmitri calls.

"Stuff's on the counter."

"Bastard."

Ivan carries his snack to the basement and turns on the television. When Dmitri brings down his own sandwich, they watch a Dr. Who rerun in companionable silence. Satisfied, Ivan drowses in his chair, drifting in and out to the sound of the Doctor's voice.

The rattling of the garage door rouses him.

"Did you clean up the counter?" Ivan asks Dmitri.

Dmitri flips him a middle finger.

Ivan grabs Dmitri's plate and glass and legs it upstairs to get the dishes in the dishwasher before his stepfather sees the mess.

The counter is spotless.

Valeriya is freaking out about something, almost screeching; her father is talking over top of her in his faux-reasonable voice—the one that implies he is infinitely calm but, as Ivan knows from experience, actually means he's nearing the end of his tether.

"We'll figure it out, Val. Mom's not the only one who's capable."

"Yes, she is! She's the only one who ever does it! I'm not letting you do it for the first time so I go to the recital looking like a freak!"

Ivan takes the two grocery bags his step-father holds out to him.

"Thanks, son." Turning to Valeriya, he puts both hands firmly on her shoulders. "You need to calm down."

"I can't! I can't get ready! There's no one to do my hair if she doesn't come home soon! Everything is *ruined*!"

"It will get done, I promise. Just go get your leotard on now. Ivan, where's your brother?"

"Downstairs."

"BUT, DAD!"

"Valeriya! Go!"

While they argue, Ivan quietly starts putting away the groceries, hoping to score a few brownie points with his stepfather.

When Val is wailing in her room, Ivan asks, "Anything I can do to help?"

"Only if you know how to braid hair."

"I can do that."

His stepfather looks surprised. "You can?"

Ivan grabs a lock of his hair and demonstrates.

"Huh. Didn't know that. You've saved my ass. Dmitri! Can you come help with dinner? Ivan, can you wear something other than black tonight? Try to dress up a bit for your sister."

"Not coming. Too much homework." He blinks against the lie.

"Seriously? Val'll be disappointed."

"*You'll* be disappointed if my grades make the university invoke the conditionalness of their conditional offer."

"Your grades aren't that bad. One night won't kill you."

"Exams are in three weeks."

His stepfather sighs. "Fine. Thanks for doing her hair for me."

Ivan notices that the circles beneath his stepfather's eyes seem to have become permanent in the last couple of months.

Valeriya sits on the edge of her bed, snuffling, her eyes red-rimmed. Ivan leans nonchalantly against the doorjamb.

"Leery, you're not dressed."

She wipes her nose on her sleeve. "I'm not going."

"Sure you are. Get your shit on. I'll do your hair." He holds out his braided lock for inspection.

She doesn't react to the profanity, but she stands up and pulls a peach-coloured garment from her dresser drawer. "Git out. I'm changing."

When she opens her bedroom door again, she is about to smear mucus on her arm once more, but Ivan catches her elbow. "Use a kleenex. That's disgusting. How do you want your hair?"

"Like a crown."

"Where're your hair things?"

He sits her on her straight-backed desk chair, where her feet still dangle a centimetre above the floor. Efficiently, he combs the knots from her wavy brown hair and brushes it smooth, parts it down the middle of her skull. She watches his every move in the mirror, without comment. His fingers plait two braids down her back.

"This is going to take a lot of hairpins. Sit still so I don't stab you."

Obediently, she freezes as he fastens the braids over the top of her head.

"There, princess. How's that crown?"

She leaps from the chair and leans close to the mirror. "Good."

"Shake your head. Will it stay? Do a couple of spins and jumps."

He's treated to a short display of her dancing abilities.

"Yeah, it's good."

"There ya go. Now go help Dad set the table. No more whining at him. Be a good Leery."

To keep up appearances, Ivan goes straight into his room and spreads some school books over the bed. Idly, he picks up the history textbook and flips to Chapter Seven.

By the time his mother comes home and dinner is announced, Ivan has finished his homework. He slouches on his bed with a book of Kerouac's poems that he borrowed from his English teacher.

After dinner, as Dmitri ties his polished shoes and smooths his hair, Ivan stands in the front hall, history textbook conspicuous in his hands.

"Good luck, Leery!" he calls from the front door. She's in the car, busy putting on her seatbelt. She doesn't acknowledge him, but his mother waves from the front seat.

He closes the front door behind Dmitri, locks it and checks the back door to make sure it's locked, too.

He wishes Lin weren't working, that he could see her, spend some time alone with her.

She always smells like sweet fruit and candy, with an undertone of flowers. Her general irreverence drew his attention and still pleasantly surprises him; a steady base of kindness is what keeps his attention, as well as her constant affection.

The best feeling—the one he conjures when the world is closing in on him—is her arms locked around his waist and her face tucked against his neck. When he puts his arms around her, crossing them over her back, he feels masculine and invincible, even though he's only a few centimetres taller than her.

He can't depend on her words, though. Despite being always kind, she avoids committing, especially when pressed.

"What do you like about me?" he asked one evening as they watched Netflix in her parents' living room.

"Absolutely nothing," she replied, feeding him a piece of buttered popcorn with delicate fingertips. "You're a total waste of my time and energy, and I'm dumping you for the captain of the football team."

"The one with the acne?"

"That's the one."

Getting no words of comfort, he settles for craving the embraces she gives, lets himself receive the heat of her body.

In the golden evening light, the hunger is a taste on his tongue; an ache in his upper arms; a thin edge of tension in his inner thighs.

Five minutes in the bathroom won't be enough to satisfy this.

His brain is an animal. He can think of nothing else. With a grunt, he rolls off his bed and stumbles over to his desk.

After staring at his browser's search bar for a moment, he types "Asian girls", thinking about Lin's curtain of hair and slender hips, her collarbone jutting above the neckline of her blouse.

The images that pop up are mostly faces. There's nothing that appeals to him. He needs more.

He adds "body" to the search.

That's more like it.

He scans the options: big eyes and small mouth, sleeveless white shirts with the top buttons undone, hair up, hair down, seductive breasts.

Standing out in the sea of flesh tones, the primary colours of the outfit catch his eye, and a thrill runs through his body before he realises exactly what he's looking at.

It annoys him when these images slip through the filters. Once his brain sees it, it gets hooked by the idea and won't let it go. He can tell by the way his body reacted so quickly that a thousand Lins wouldn't be able to give him what he wants now.

He has made rules about this. If he can't get it out of his head, he limits himself to two images: the first is a chipped, flaking fresco from Pompeii; the second is Pagliei's *Naiads* from 1881.

He tells himself he should go into the living room and get the art books. His family thinks nothing of him looking at them—and he has the visual arts project as an excuse.

The online photo whispers to him.

The picture is an old one, the sort he's seen in his parents' family albums that document lives by milestones and annual celebrations.

The girl—six or seven years old—is standing in a bedroom. It's a normal child's bedroom, with brightly-coloured bedclothes and about a hundred stuffed animals. Outside the window is a dusting of snow on a bare tree, and there are white cut-paper snowflakes taped haphazardly to the windowpane. The girl is the focal point of the shot. She wears a Wonder Woman undershirt and underpants set, and has a large, shiny, red Christmas bow stuck to the top of her head. Her arms are crossed over her chest, and her right hip juts saucily towards the viewer, so a wedge of pristine flesh is visible above the bright blue waistband of the pants. Her head is turned: she glowers from behind a wedge of messy hair. Her tongue sticks out between rose-bud lips.

He inhales sharply.

There have been warnings about images like this. If he were to click on this image, it would be easy, he suspects, to find other images like this. There would be more children in colourful underwear, "naturist" photos of families which could be cropped to remove the nude adults.

His finger hits the mouse, taking him to the website. The Wonder Woman girl's image is close to the top of the page, just below a photo of a blonde girl playing dress-up in her mother's negligee. Below Wonder Woman girl are photos of children and young teens in various states of undress, including completely naked.

Ivan quickly clicks the back button, returning to the safety of his browser's image search, and puts his hands on his thighs.

The left side of his chest feels shaky, fluttery, but his brain promises emotions, release, satisfaction like he's never had before, like he's craved for years.

The girl wouldn't know any different.

The girl—girl? No, he can tell from the hairstyle and clothing that this girl would now be a woman of perfectly legal age. Any harm caused by the photo has been done;

anything he, Ivan, does will be immaterial. Like taking pleasure in the 2 000-year-old fresco.

This girl might even be dead. Not everyone lives past the age of thirty, even. People get ill. People have accidents.

He has considered this before. Would he be okay with someone using an old photo of him, when he was a kid? Sure, he'd be down with that. It's just a photograph. No one abused him. As with this image, any pictures of him weren't meant to be sexual, so it's okay. It's fine.

But the girl...?

Did she consent?

She must have. Everyone has those photos of themselves. Parents haul them out and show them to everyone, on every birthday: children running naked in the backyard, playing with bubbles and rubber ducks in the bath.

Ivan closes his eyes and mentally ages the girl to Lin's age. Her hair thickens, straightens; her cheeks lengthen and cheekbones appear. Her tiny shoulders extend to support long, slender arms that could easily encircle his body.

Her lips thin out.

Her eyes are rimmed with eyeliner, her lashes lengthened with mascara.

Another glance at the image erases the new image of Lin, refreshing the urgency in the pit of his stomach.

His hands slide down his thighs, closer to his knees.

Part of his brain still tries to imagine the pleasures that could be found, but the rest of his brain slams on the brakes.

His palms sweat.

The fluttering in his chest turns to thudding.

His throat is dry; he swallows the saliva that has collected in his mouth.

A chill runs through him.

No.

He's not that person.

She is a person—or was.

He clicks on the drop-down menu and selects "report image".

He closes the browser and slowly lowers the lid to the laptop.

Curled up on his bed, facing the wall, he jams his cold hands between his knees.

Then he reaches for his phone. He texts Lin, knowing she's still at work and won't even have a break for another fifty-six minutes.

love u

He opens the app for his special chat room.

Maskedman: hey there

'sup?

MAP Chat: Friendship

NotYourMother: We have a new member

    Feel free to introduce yourself

Bramstoker: straight white male

    pedo GL

    almost an adult

    @bunnyboy's friend

Oskar: Welcome, Bram Stoker

DontGimmeLolita: How did u 2 meet

Bramstoker: met on another chat

    took us a while to figure out we lived in the same city

NotHumbert: I know what you mean...

    Welcome, @BramStoker. I take it you like Gothic literature?

    @PedoProud will be thrilled.

BramStoker: the book is okay but i really just like vampires

    they're my monster of choice

PedoProud: Damn. I thought @Oskar and I would have another reader in the group

bunnyboy: why would i make friends with a nerd

BramStoker: wont help ur soccer skills for sure

Oskar: It would do you a world of good to make friends with a variety of people, Bunny Boy. That is how we learn.

DontGimmeLolita: wait a second

What did you say back there, @NotHumbert

NotHumbert: Back where?

DontGimmeLolita: Quote: @NotHumbert: *I know what you mean...*

NotHumbert: Um...

PedoProud: I think we can tell them.

@NotHumbert and I have been dating for a couple of months.

(It turns out he's really hot!)

DontGimmeLolita: LOL!!!

NotHumbert: *blush*

NotYourMother: That's awesome

Oskar: Felicitations to you both, Not Humbert and Pedo Proud.

PedoProud: Thanks. :)

BramStoker: you live in the same place?

NotHumbert: Not even in the same country.

We're geographically close, though, so it won't be hard to meet up.

PedoProud: We've only met by video.

NotYourMother: Taking a risk.

PedoProud: It was worth the risk, in my opinion.

NotHumbert: In my opinion too. We've got to trust someone at some point.

DontGimmeLolita: online friendships are good

Real life friendships are better

We need more of those.

bunnyboy: ur a good matchmaker @NotYourMother

Ryan

Ryan wakes facing the half-light of a grey Saturday morning.

"Sure you're going golfing?" Liza mutters into her pillow.

Ryan makes a non-committal noise and turns to face her. Her dark, wiry hair stands up from the pillow, giving her a wild, witchy look. He reaches out to pull gently at a tuft, then kisses her to make up for it.

She raises an eyebrow but kisses him back. "Any sounds from the kids?"

"'Course not. It's just past 8:00."

"Have I mentioned how much I love teenagers?"

"You only love them when they're sleeping. You're not so fond of them when you look at the grocery bill." He kisses her again, on her silky cheek this time, lingering to take in her warm scent. "Wanna lock the door and pretend we're teenagers again?"

"Uh-huh. For sure."

As he languidly makes love with his wife, Ryan keeps an ear cocked for footsteps and opening doors, even though they can probably count on at least two more hours to themselves. He still lives in fear of a repeat of the day—thirteen years ago—when their four-year-old walked in on them and they'd had to lie about a tickle fight.

What he really fears now is the social-media critique of his bedroom skills.

Though he longs to fall back to sleep with his head on Liza's soft breasts, he wraps his arms and legs around her, holding her tightly.

"Saturday mornings are good," she purrs, breathing on his chest hair, making him suddenly aware of her lips.

"Very good."

"What're you guys gonna do if it does rain today?"

"Dunno. We'll figure something out. Maybe just play in the rain. Not so crowded then."

"Hmm."

"What are you doing today?"

"Michael's working, and Chris and Thom are going to the twins' place for some epic video game session. I think I'll go shopping, maybe see a movie."

"By yourself?"

"Yeah."

"I thought you ladies were having girls' day tomorrow. Aren't you gonna see a movie then?"

"They only like chick-flicks. I want to see that documentary on addiction."

"Huh."

"Unless you want to see it with me?"

"No action, no sex... nah, but thanks for thinking of me."

"I'm home for the boys in the late afternoon, so Alia can do errands without coming home to find her house on fire. You coming home for dinner?"

"Hadn't made any other plans. Want us to hunt down and kill something?"

"I'll do it. Roberto's staying?"

"That okay?"

"Sure. Always."

Sleep threatens to overcome him. He shakes himself, draws a finger up and down her spine. "Coffee?"

"Yeah."

As the coffee burbles into the pot, Ryan whisks together some pancake batter. His phone bleeps a text alert.

Roberto: *Got a proposal for ya*

Ryan: *Whuzzat?*

Roberto: *From a friend*

Bringing the info with me

Ryan: *Kk*

Not ready yet tho

Roberto: *Me 2 neither*

Get ready

There are voices from the bedrooms. Ryan hears feet thudding down the stairs, and the bathroom door slams shut. He pours a mug of coffee, adds four spoonfuls of sugar and enough coffee cream so the liquid is barely beige, and holds it out as Michael comes into the kitchen.

"Morning, son."

"Humph."

"Working today?"

"At 12:30."

Ryan abandons the attempted conversation and pours batter circles on the griddle. Through the kitchen window, he can see the sky darkening. There's a heaviness to the air, though it's still cool.

He cracks the patio door open for fresh air and flips on the overhead light.

Michael blinks and squints at him. Ryan responds with a nod at the coffee mug; Michael takes another sip.

The ceiling above the kitchen shudders with a thump, then with another one, and one final thump. The twins' voices are drowned out by a sudden swell of hip-hop, and Liza's voice bellows above the cacophony. There are more thuds, door slams, unintelligible calls in one voice and then another.

Michael frowns at his mug.

Ryan flips the pancakes and the sausages. Using the spatula to conduct, he orchestrates the arrival of the rest of his family and the chaotic beginning of breakfast: more feet thundering down the stairs, the clinking and clanking of dishes, the voices all talking over each other, the twins sliding into home plate as they vie for the single high-backed chair at the head of the table beneath the van Gogh sunflower print.

"Christopher." The spatula is a brandished weapon. "You had it at dinner. It's Thom's turn. Christ, you're like a couple of children."

Chris gets out of the chair with a slap at his brother's arm. Thom sticks his tongue out.

"Yeah," Michael echoes. "*Children*."

With a pleading look, Liza holds three plates in front of Ryan. He flips two pancakes and two sausages onto each plate.

He predicts it: twenty-two seconds until they've finished fighting over the syrup and picked up their forks. Blessed silence, except for the quiet sizzling of frying food.

He hands Liza a light blue mug of black coffee. When she sits at the table, the surface of the coffee reflects the white overhead light.

The minute he sees the boys' wolfing starting to slow, he adds a plate of fresh fruit and cheese to the table. Liza absent-mindedly nibbles a pear slice. There's a sheen on the thin stripe of green skin pausing against the deep pink of her lips.

"Thom," Michael grunts, "send the plums this way."

Thom shoves the plate, scraping it over the wooden tabletop.

"Thomas," his mother warns.

Ryan pours another batch of pancakes and adds a few more sausages to the griddle. "Leave some for Roberto. He'll be here soon."

"MAP day?" Thom asks.

"Yep."

"And how are the MAPs acknowledging their sexuality today?"

"Hitting little balls with big sticks."

265

"Yusuf and Amir are coming over, too," Chris mumbles to his plate.

"They need breakfast?"

"Probably. I dunno."

Shrugging, Ryan adds a couple of extra circles of batter in the space beside the sausages.

Liza yawns. "We should book the plane tickets for Christmas."

"I thought you booked those weeks ago?"

"Meant to."

"So, where's the money? What came out of the savings account?" He raises an eyebrow and tries to keep the irritation out of his voice.

"Had to use it to pay the taxes. I used the tax money for the landscapers."

The kids look back and forth between Liza and Ryan, absorbing the tennis game of adulthood.

Ryan takes a couple of sips of coffee before responding. "Okay. Take it out of the chequing account. I'll move things around on Monday."

The doorbell rings just as Ryan sees two long, lithe figures leaping the back fence and sliding across the dewy lawn to press their faces against the glass patio doors. Chris tips his chair back to slide the door open for the other set of twins, and Michael gets up to let Roberto in the front door.

After making sure Yusuf is the one to take his seat, Thom goes to the dining room to bring in three more chairs.

Again, there's the chaos of voices and crockery, the chiming of silverware. Ryan fills plates and glasses, greeting Roberto with a gentle slap on the shoulder so he doesn't interrupt the conversation Roberto's already started with Michael.

"...got three more for you to proofread, if you're okay with that."

"Yeah, sure. This week's good. Mid-terms don't start for another month. Now's a good time."

"Awesome. Thanks. I'll email them to you tonight. No rush. I also got... nah, gotta talk to your dad about that first."

"About what?"

"Nothing. I'll tell you later."

"Well, now I'm on tenterhooks."

"*Tenterhooks*. Are you sure you're only seventeen?"

Liza grins proudly. "That's my English major."

"Keep up with the programme, old man. Us teenagers are so totally worldly right now."

Within fifteen minutes, the two sets of twins have devoured all they can hold and are headed back over the fence to spend the day taking out the virtual zombie population, and Michael has retreated upstairs to get ready for work.

Roberto glances at Ryan's outfit. "Very chic."

"I thought so." He smooths the soft fabric of his pyjama pants and t-shirt. Roberto looks sophisticated in black trousers and a white-and-black polo shirt. "What did you want to show me?"

"Later." Roberto looks out the window. "Let's see if we can get a round in before the rain."

Ryan flings his clubs into Roberto's tiny hatchback. Sidney Bechet plays as Roberto turns on the car.

"Want something different?"

"Nah, 'salright. I'm okay with listening to your shit music for a short drive. I'll make you listen to something real later."

"Some little boy band crap?"

"Drake's a *man*."

"I'll take your word for it, but Sidney was a *real* man."

They drive along the quiet highway by the lake. The huge trees are still green, though here and there they're starting to look pale at the top. At the bend in the road, both men automatically look towards the water, at the little choppy grey waves with white heads.

Roberto turns into the parking lot of the country club. "I dunno, man. Looks like the only people here are the ones that have to be."

"It's not raining yet. Let's see what happens."

"Quiet today?" Roberto asks as he signs his name.

The attendant taps keys on the computer keyboard. "There are a couple of diehards like you two out there. It hasn't rained yet, so the green is still good."

Out the wall-sized window, Ryan can't see any of the diehards. Diehards, he thinks, usually get out on the green pretty early in the morning. Diehards don't postpone golfing until almost noon.

He yawns and sets his bag into the back of a golf cart.

The sky starts spitting when they're at the second hole, and it's becoming annoying by the fourth. Ryan looks up.

"You're gonna drown, doing that." Roberto drapes his towel over his head. "Let's go. I've got a better idea."

Back in the car, watching the splattering on the windshield, Ryan wipes his hands over the water spots on his navy trousers. "What's the better idea?"

270

"You'll see. Don't worry, you can still hit things."

Ryan smiles wryly and nods. "Good thing you know me so well, sir."

Beneath the white dome that glares even in the rain, the men don batting helmets and choose their bats. Ryan feels energy surge through his body into his brain. He's alert, impatient to get to his net.

"Good idea—batting cages," he acknowledges.

"Thought it might do, if the great outdoors won't co-operate."

Ryan hits the button. The flight of the first ball surprises him. He sees it almost in slow motion, coming at him as if it's got some personal issues with him: hitting it is a defensive instinct. The ball connects with the bat but slides along the top of it and lands just a few metres in front of him.

He's ready for the next one. It cracks perfectly on the bat and flies right back from where it came. He's a little disappointed that he can't watch it land, but he doesn't want to miss the next ball. Fixing his stance, he prepares for the third attack, which he sends in the same direction.

When he finishes his first set, he glances at Roberto in the net beside him. A lefty, Roberto has his back to Ryan, but Ryan can see part of the satisfied expression as Roberto hits his last ball.

"Freakin' nailed it." Ryan grins.

"Round two."

Towards the end of the hour, Ryan feels his shoulders loosen, though he hadn't noticed they were tight. Adrenaline buzzes through his muscles, and his brain feels as though he's high on something.

By the time they leave the sports dome, the rain has stopped and billowing grey clouds race each other.

"Beer?" Ryan asks the sky.

"For sure."

"The game started fifteen minutes ago, but the kids might be back soon."

"The bar it is, then."

They park the car at Ryan's house and walk the three blocks to the bar. The wet wind forces them to huddle into their coats, hands jammed in their pockets; they march along without talking. With a block to go, Roberto raises his head.

"Enough of this." He breaks into a jog.

Ryan starts jogging with him, pushing against the wind.

When Roberto yanks open the door, Ryan can feel the warmth waft out of the bar.

Along with a roomful of other people, Ryan and Roberto sip steadily at a couple of pints while cursing and cheering at the TV screen. As the alcohol erases the last bits of tension, the game starts to get interesting. Ryan is hooked by the movements of the players, the speed of the ball as it skitters and soars across the field. Neither of the teams are his favourite, so he starts cheering for the underdogs. With the final goal, he sinks back in his chair, groaning along with the rest of the losers.

Roberto slams his glass down on the tabletop and raises a victory fist.

They stride home, wind at their backs, collars up against the driving rain, cursing the damage to their shoes.

In the foyer, they grin at each other like small children as they drip on the mat.

"Hold tight," Ryan says. "I'll get towels."

When he returns, Roberto is staring at the folding door on the coat closet. "This thing is never closed."

"It's broken."

"How long's it been broken?"

Ryan shrugs. "Five years?"

"Get your tools. We're going to be productive."

When Liza returns with grocery sacks and a small cream-coloured shopping bag with gold lettering, the men have the folding door in pieces on the hallway floor. "Oh, good. Carnage."

"We're being useful." Ryan kisses her cheek.

"Would the handymen like tea?"

Ryan glances at Roberto as he replies to her. "Would you mind putting on the coffee pot while you're making tea?"

They join Liza in the kitchen, where she's getting out mugs while humming to something on her iPod.

"The door, she closes!" Ryan announces.

"Finally. That thing only broke, what, a decade ago?"

"Nah, not that long... was it?"

They hear voices coming from the backyard and turn to see four boys leaping over the fence. The teenagers seem to be yelling at each other about some violent encounter Ryan sincerely hopes is merely part of a video game. Without acknowledging the adults, the kids stomp through the kitchen and down the basement stairs.

Liza stands on the back porch to wave across the yard to the twins' mother. "I'll send them back after dinner!"

The air from the backyard makes Liza shiver as she slides the door shut.

"Let me take some cookies downstairs for the savage beasts. Then we can have coffee in peace." She loads a tray with a full package of digestive biscuits and some soda cans, then adds a bowl of potato chips for good measure.

"Can you open the door for me, Roberto?"

He jumps up from his chair. "Want me to take that?"

"I'm good, thanks."

He flicks on the light switch for her, and the kids yell about the glare on their screen.

"I'll turn it off in a second, for heaven's sake!" she placates. "I come bearing food!"

Roberto returns to his chair and takes a sip of coffee.

"So, what's this thing you wanted to talk about?"

"Yeah, right. I guess now is a good time. Hold on while I get my bag. I left it in the front hall."

Liza comes up the basement stairs, turns off the light switch and firmly closes the basement door on bellows of "Arrrrgh!" and "Behind you! Get him!". She slides into her chair beside Ryan and reaches for a cookie. "What's up?"

Roberto slips a tablet from his bag and turns it on. "A few days ago, I had an idea, and I want to run it by you two. Ryan, how'd you feel about using your Twitter and Medium to take on sex travel?" He hands the tablet to Ryan and Liza, open at a graphic organiser.

"What do you want to do?" Liza asks, looking at the screen.

"There's lots of anti-contact MAPs doing the general *here's-a-pedo* thing. I think I want to get specifically into anti-child porn and anti-child sex travel."

Ryan scrolls through the proposal. "There are a couple of guys who already do anti-CP. I guess it's a good idea."

"I really want to do this. I feel like I'm just doing the same thing over and over: *Yes, it's an orientation; No, I don't fantasise about that.* I want to do something concrete—make a difference." Roberto's voice gets a little louder, faster, and his eyes brighten. "If I actually *do* something, *help* someone, *save* someone, there's some purpose to putting up with all the shit from the trolls. Right now, all

I get is abuse. I want a reason to get out of bed in the morning. No one is going to have a problem with me trying to stop it. I'll work with all the anti-CP organisations. Actually *do* something."

Liza looks up. "What are the risks?"

"No more than anything else we do."

"I want to do a website, maybe get Michael to help me write the content. I'd pay him, of course," Roberto adds. "I want to do this properly—eventually get donations and do talks and stuff."

"How're you gonna do talks?"

"Maybe videos with my face obscured. Maybe I'll just go do it live."

Ryan exchanges a look with his wife. "You know I can't do that. I can't take that risk. I've got the kids and Liza to think about."

"Yeah, yeah, I know. I knew that. I didn't expect *you* to do that stuff, just help with the website and the writing, re-Tweet some stuff. I don't even know if I'll do it for sure. Just thinking about it."

Liza is gripping Ryan's thigh a little too hard. "It's a good concept, Roberto. It's something that really needs to be talked about, but I just want to be sure you two are safe."

"I know, I know. I won't do anything that'll put you guys in jeopardy."

"I think you doing anything live puts us in jeopardy." The tendons in Ryan's neck are standing out. "If they figure out where you live, they'll easily associate you with us. They'll know you spend time here. They'll know you spend time with Michael. I mean, it's great that you and Michael are close, but for Christ's sake, if they go after Michael..." He exhales sharply. "I've gotta put some limits on it. If you want to do anything with your real voice or your face, we'll have to stop hanging out. I'll have to publicly denounce you. Sorry, mate, but my family comes first."

"Okay. Okay." Roberto holds up a hand. "I said I won't do anything that might hurt you. That's why I wanted to run this by you first."

Liza sits back and crosses her arms. "Thank you."

Roberto reaches out to take the tablet back, but Ryan grips the edges. "No, don't get me wrong. I think it's a good idea. I will probably help you."

Liza looks down at her lap as Roberto lets go of the tablet.

"You're right," Ryan says a little more calmly. "There's lots of us out there on the internet now. It'd be a good thing to cast the nets a little wider, see if we can't maybe convert some sex travellers to our way of thinking, prevent some people from going to Thailand and stuff. If we combine it with anti-child porn, we'll be covering a lot of ground."

Roberto nods.

"But," Ryan continues, "we use our pseudonyms and avatars. Only."

Roberto nods again.

"Are you guys sure about this?" Liza speaks softly and worries the edge of her thumbnail.

"Honey, if we stay hidden... I don't think it's any more of a risk than we take now. And it feels like a moral obligation, kind of. If I chicken out just because of what might happen, what sort of a person am I?

"What risks do you see if we just use avatars?" Roberto asks.

She's silent for a moment. "I suppose that's nothing new, yeah."

Roberto looks to Ryan. "What if we think about it for a week and then decide?"

"'Cause then there are kids at risk for another week," Ryan sighs. "The longer before people end it, the more kids get hurt."

"Can I ask Michael to proofread for the website? I can do the writing, if you don't want to involve him."

"As long as it doesn't cut into his homework time." Liza gets up to fetch the coffee pot. She refills her cup first, then offers the pot to the other two.

Outside, the clouds are beginning to break; on the horizon, the edges of the clouds are tinged with red. The wind is crisp.

The light in the kitchen, where Ryan and Roberto sit by the window, is a calm pinkish-grey. By the stove, Liza is dark gold in the light from above the range.

By the time the lasagnes are ready, Michael has returned from work and joined the four boys in the basement. Roberto is standing at the kitchen island, assembling an elegant salad that will be destroyed the moment the boys sit down, while Liza sets the table and Ryan unwraps the hot loaf of garlic bread.

"Boys! Dinner's ready!"

Christopher bellows up the stairs. "Can Yusuf and Amir stay?"

"I cleared it with their mother yesterday. Get with the schedule, guys."

Ryan stands as the rest of them shuffle into their chairs. "Actually," he says, laying down the serving utensils. "How'd you guys feel about saying grace, first?"

"Seriously, Dad? We haven't done that since we were kids."

Liza holds her hands out. "I think it's a good idea. We've got a lot to be thankful for at this table."

Taking one of Liza's hands and one of Roberto's, Ryan feels his mind start to spin. He tries to sort through it for a few seconds, and then looks at Roberto.

With a slight tilt of his head in acknowledgement, Roberto opens his mouth to pray.

The author would like to thank the members of the various anti-contact, non-offending MAP communities, especially Ender. Many thanks to the beta-readers for looking past the "ick factor" and to my editor.

Salmacis' Press

www.salmacispress.ca

Made in the USA
Columbia, SC
20 October 2023